———————————— ★ ————————————

"You're here to identify the drowning victim?" he asked.

"I'm praying that I can't, but I'm afraid I do know her."

"If you'll wait just a moment, please." He went into the next room, and in a few minutes the curtains on the window parted and a gurney holding a draped form was on the other side of the glass. I clenched my jaw and willed myself not to faint or cry out or otherwise make a fool of myself. Caronis stood close to me; I suppose he suspected that he might have to catch me.

After a second's hesitation, the man pulled the sheet down to reveal a face. Although it was white and puffy, and her hair was matted about her head in slick tendrils like auburn seaweed, there was no doubt it was Beth.

"Oh, no!" I cried out before I realized I'd spoken. I was unprepared for the strong sense of loss I felt.

"You know her then," Caronis said.

"It's Beth Wilkinson. I barely know her."

"All right. Let's go back to the station. You can tell me everything you know."

———————————— ★ ————————————

SQUALL LINE
NANCY GOTTER GATES

WORLDWIDE®

TORONTO • NEW YORK • LONDON
AMSTERDAM • PARIS • SYDNEY • HAMBURG
STOCKHOLM • ATHENS • TOKYO • MILAN
MADRID • WARSAW • BUDAPEST • AUCKLAND

Recycling programs
for this product may
not exist in your area.

A Worldwide Mystery/December 2011

First published by Alabaster Book Publishers

ISBN-13: 978-0-373-26780-4

Copyright © 2010 by Nancy Gotter Gates

Printed in U.S.A.

Thanks to Detectives Gary Selzer and Bob Reou
of the Criminal Investigation Division of
the Sarasota Police Department, Dory Lock and
Jennifer Coburn of the Ringling School of Art,
and Pete Lindeman of Sarasota Memorial Hospital.

ONE

WHEN I HEARD THE MAN'S voice, for one brief heart-stopping moment I thought it was Paul. Then reality set in—as it always does. Paul died just over a year ago, but every now and then I'll forget for just an instant. And when I realize my mistake, it always brings a wave of sorrow as the truth comes flooding back. I hoped that someday soon I could get past that point and, though his memory will always occupy a significant place in my heart, be able to relegate it to a past life that no longer exists.

The rhythmic murmur of the waves and the warmth of the sun must have lulled me to sleep. I was stretched out on my beach towel in shorts and a tee and had closed my eyes after reading the *Herald-Tribune*. I spend time on Crescent Beach early every morning, directly below my eleventh-floor condo at La Hacienda on Siesta Key, a bridge-span away from Sarasota. I'm so fair-skinned I need to avoid the midday sun and slather on sunscreen repeatedly. While I hunt for shells I wear a broad-brimmed hat, which now lay on the sand beside me.

"Mind if I join you?" The voice penetrated my consciousness and I opened my eyes, startled into wakefulness. I felt disoriented for a few seconds, not sure where

I was or the time of day. Finally I realized there was a stranger sitting close beside me. I sat up immediately.

"Sorry if I alarmed you," he said. I could tell he was tall, even though he was sitting. He appeared to be in his late fifties, my age, and was wearing jeans, a T-shirt with a Sarasota logo and running shoes. His full head of hair was a salt-and-pepper mix and his blue eyes were guileless. "I'm Tom. And you're...?"

I was a little apprehensive that he was sitting next to me when there were long stretches of nearly empty sand on either side of us. If I'd been awake, I wouldn't have been taken so by surprise.

"Emma," I told him, steeling myself for some kind of pass. I suppose it would have been flattering at my age, but I wasn't in the mood for it.

As if he read my mind he said, "I'm not trying to be fresh, Emma. Honestly." He smiled and looked embarrassed—and shy. He seemed younger when he grinned like that. "I was looking for someone on the beach I could ask a favor of." He raised his eyebrows in question like a child who wants to influence his mother favorably. It gave him an aura of ingenuousness which I have to admit was appealing. He seemed anything but threatening when he smiled.

"Such as?"

"Let me explain." He leaned back casually on both elbows. "I've been staying on Siesta Key for the past week at the Sand Dune—" he pointed up the beach toward one of the high-rises closer to the center of Siesta Village "—and I've been walking the length of the beach every day about noon. I generally sleep late and don't get up much before that." He grinned sheepishly as though confessing his sins. "There's a young woman down by Point of Rocks every day who's working on a painting, a view of the beach. Have you by any chance seen her?"

"Yes, as a matter of fact, I have. Seems quite talented." Point of Rocks is about a half mile away at the south end of Crescent Beach, a frequent round-trip walk for me. I have a deep fear of water, so it might seem ludicrous for me to be living next to the Gulf, but nothing soothes my spirit more than a walk along its edge. The mere anticipation of finding a special seashell or the chance to watch the shorebirds scurry about can add a few moments of delight to my day. These moments are what give me the peace and courage to keep going without Paul.

"Well, I always stop there a few minutes to rest and to see how her painting is coming. We usually talk a bit."

"I've chatted with her, too. She's a lovely young woman."

Mr. Whoever smiled broadly again, injecting another dose of charm to keep me interested. "Right, right. I told her I knew of a great little gallery back home in Rochester that I'm sure would carry her paintings. People get so weary of snow that they buy paintings of Florida beaches to cheer themselves up."

"Minnesota?"

"New York. Lake effect, you know. We get dumped

on with several feet of the stuff each winter because we're near the lake."

I took off my sunglasses and cleaned them with a corner of the towel, waiting for him to continue. What on earth did all this have to do with me?

"I didn't know the address of the gallery or the owner's name," he continued. "But last night I had to call my brother in Rochester, and he got me the information from the yellow pages. I wanted to give it to her today, but something has come up and I have to leave a day early. I've got a ten-fifteen flight this morning, and I know she doesn't get out on the beach until noon or so."

"So, you want me to go down there this afternoon and give her the name and address."

"Would you mind? You'd be doing both of us a favor. She might find a good outlet for her work there."

I thought about it for a minute. I had no real plans for the day other than grocery shopping and a trip to the library. And I quite admired her work. In fact, there had been an article in the paper about her a week or so earlier, about how she lived with her elderly grandmother on Casey Key and took a few hours each day to paint on Siesta Key, which is one island north of Casey. I remembered her first name was Beth, but I couldn't remember her last name. "Sure, I'll do it."

"You're a good sport." He stood up, worked something out of his hip pocket and handed it to me. It was a folded white envelope with "Beth" written on the front of it. "Thanks so much. I know she'll appreciate it."

I took it and laid it on top of the newspaper next to my bifocals. "Going back to Rochester?"

"Unfortunately," he said, dusting the sand from the seat of his jeans. "Well, gotta go. Thanks again." He gave me one last dazzling smile and headed north toward the village at a lazy pace.

I watched him till he was out of sight and then gathered my things and went back to the condo. I had to pass by the pool where Paul would have been taking his morning swim. It still hurt to look at the empty expanse of water that lapped softly against the bright blue sides.

I took the elevator to our two-bedroom condominium where we'd lived only six months when Paul died suddenly of a heart attack while jogging on Crescent Beach. He was fifty-nine and he'd taken early retirement to fulfill a lifelong dream of living in Florida. I say it was Paul's dream because I was along for the ride. I never protested when we moved to Sarasota. How could I deny him the thing he'd worked so long and hard for? But it meant leaving all my friends in Columbus behind, which was wrenching at the time. It helped that my son, Mark, had recently moved from Toledo to Tampa so I saw him occasionally. And I'd learned to love the gorgeous view of the beach and the many wonderful amenities Sarasota had to offer that made it the cultural center of Florida.

I did a few housekeeping chores, but my air-conditioned, sealed-up home doesn't need much maintenance, which suits me just fine. Housework has never been one of my favorite things, and the relaxed lifestyle here lets me get away with being slack about it. Nobody really notices a dust puppy here or there.

I showered and dressed in beige linen slacks and a pale pink tee, made out a grocery list and went out to my little silver Civic hatchback that I love in spite of the fact it has one-hundred-and-fifty-thousand-some miles. I drove down Midnight Pass Road past block after block of towering condominium buildings that obscured my view of the Gulf. Even though it has been widened to three lanes to allow a turn lane, the road more often than not resembles a parking lot during season. I always worry about how quickly the island could be evacuated in the event of a hurricane.

One of the things I love most about Siesta Key is the lushness of its vegetation. On this stretch of road where it skirts the beach, the high-rises are formally landscaped. But along most of Midnight Pass and Higel Avenue, the main roads, the residential areas still have a wild, junglelike ambience where homes are concealed behind masses of live oak, Australian pine and a variety of other tropical trees and plants. At this time the Tree of Gold and the orchid tree were in bloom, adding their yellow and lavender hues to the bright bougainvillea blossoms.

I turned left at Stickney Point Road and drove across the drawbridge to Tamiami Trail where the Publix is located. To my surprise, the parking lot in front of the store wasn't as crowded as usual. I took this to be a good omen: at long last most of the snowbirds had left to go back North. I have to admit it's a relief when they leave because it means less traffic and no more waiting in long lines for the early-bird special at the restaurants.

After I'd finished shopping and the bags of groceries were stashed in the back end of the car, I headed back across Stickney Point Bridge toward the key. I hoped Beth would be on the beach now since it was almost noon. I couldn't stay there long because the frozen foods would soon start to thaw in the heat of the car. I turned left at Midnight Pass and drove the couple of blocks to Point of Rocks Road, a sleepy little two-block road lined with modest one- and two-story rental units, quite a contrast to the huge buildings on Midnight Pass. Parking is prohibited at Point of Rocks and it has only a narrow beach access, a sandy path lined with yucca and sea grape, between a small motel and a private residence. I pulled my car into a grassy space beside the path, thankful for my small car and the fact there are no curbs, and hoped I wouldn't get towed.

I took my purse, locked the car and walked down the path, wishing I was barefoot as I sank into the soft sand that quickly filled my shoes. Crescent Beach sand is as white as sugar and just as fine. To the left of the path's convergence with the beach is Point of Rocks, a remarkable natural formation of flat-topped rocks making an uneven series of steps that jut into the Gulf in a kind of ledge that marks the end of the sand. The surf has worn small basins into the surface of the rocks, creating little tide pools that capture tiny creatures and ocean detritus. It's a wonderful place to explore for shells and other treasures from the sea.

I saw Beth standing at an easel in front of a retaining wall that separates the beach from private property. Instead of looking toward the sea, she was turned so that she had a view up the length of Crescent Beach. She was wearing striped shorts, a man's shirt with the front tails tied in a knot at her waist and a large straw hat over her short auburn curls.

I walked toward her. "Beth?"

"Yes?" She was so absorbed in her work she'd apparently not heard me approach, the soft sand muffling any footsteps. She straightened up from her canvas. "Oh, hi," she said. "How are you? I'm sorry. Your name is…?"

"Emma Daniels, though I don't think I ever told you before. How's the picture coming?" I stepped beside her so I could see the painting. It was impressive. She'd captured the uniqueness of Crescent Beach: its gleaming white sand, the perfect curve that gave it its name and the sea and its gradations of color from the deep aquamarine that defined the horizon to the almost foamgreen in the shallows near the shore. It even made the row of condominiums seem attractive, though I view them as a deplorable encroachment upon nature—in spite of the fact I live in one.

"That's lovely," I said. "Looks like you're about finished."

"Thank you. I'm getting there." Beth's smile was self-deprecating. "How did you know my name? We never did actually introduce ourselves, did we? Oh, I'll bet you saw the article about me in the *Herald-Tribune*."

"I did. But I've forgotten your last name."

"Wilkinson."

"Did that article generate any new business for you? I thought the reporter did a grand job."

"I've had a couple of people come by and ask me to paint a favorite scene for them. And someone has dibs on this painting."

"Wonderful. Oh, gosh, I almost forgot. I have something for you," I said as I searched my purse for the note Tom gave me.

"You do? Oh, I'll bet you brought me a copy of the article. How nice."

"No, I didn't think to save it. Here's what I have." I handed her the envelope. "A man approached me on the beach this morning, said he wanted you to have this information about some gallery in Rochester, New York. Said he promised it to you."

Beth looked puzzled. "What gallery? Who was this man?"

I shrugged. "Said his name was Tom. Told me he talked to you every day this week. He got the name of the gallery from his brother last night when he called him up in Rochester, but he had to leave this morning and couldn't bring it to you himself."

Beth shook her head as she opened the envelope. "That's strange. I don't remember talking to anyone about a gallery in New York." She read the contents of the note, and her face drained of color. "Oh, my God," she said. "Oh, my God!"

She sat down suddenly on the sand and buried her face in her hands.

TWO

"WHAT IS IT?" I SQUATTED down next to Beth, frantic to help, but not having the remotest idea what was wrong. Beth was now staring out to sea, a look of utter shock in her eyes. She sat like that, unresponsive, for a couple of minutes before beginning to take in deep, desperate breaths. "Is there anything I can do?" I felt utterly powerless and was truly frightened by her reaction.

She shook her head vehemently, indicating she wanted no help from me. In fact, she waved me away.

But I wouldn't leave. I sat down beside her. "I can't leave you like this, Beth. I'm going to at least sit here until you feel better."

There were a couple of beachgoers looking for shells around the rocks and three more sitting or lying on the beach not far away. They all were staring at the two of us with open curiosity. But Beth seemed unaware of them.

Finally tears began coursing slowly down her cheeks. She wiped them away, leaving a blue smudge from some paint on her right hand. But she seemed unable to function, almost as if she'd been paralyzed into inaction. Then suddenly she jumped up and began throwing her brushes, paints and palette that were lying on a small folding stool into a wooden box. She slammed the lid shut, took the painting and leaned it against the stool while folding up the aluminum easel. She started to gather it all together when suddenly she stopped and put them down again. I noticed her hands were trembling violently.

"Oh, God, what'll I do?" Beth's voice was panicky, her expression one of utter desolation.

I had gotten up when Beth did, watching helplessly as she prepared to leave. Now I put my arm around her shoulders to comfort her. "Please let me help. Whatever it is." Something in the note had triggered her distress, and I was the one who had delivered it, which put me squarely in the middle of whatever was going on.

She shook off my arm, pointed her finger at me and stared at me with hatred in her eyes. "Did you really think you'd get away with it?" she asked, bitterness in her voice.

"Get away with what?" I hadn't the slightest notion of what she was talking about. Whatever was in that note, she obviously believed I had written it. "Beth, I honestly thought that note was exactly what Tom told me it was. I'm not making up a story. Why would I do that?"

Beth bit her lip, working hard to keep her emotions under control. She looked at me for a long while as if trying to come to some decision. At last she said in almost a whisper, "I hope to God you're telling the truth, Emma, because I do need some help." She opened the wooden box where she'd put the envelope and handed it to me.

The note had been written on a computer and printed in ubiquitous Times Roman typeface. "We know how fond you are of your grandmother, Nan Southard. She is in our hands right now. If you really care about her you'll be home this afternoon at three o'clock. We'll call you with further instructions then. If you call the cops, something bad will happen to her. She's safe enough right now, but if you want to keep her that way, you'd better do what we tell you."

I was as stunned as Beth had been. To think I'd been the bearer of such a cruel and shocking letter. It had to be one of the lowest points in my life.

"What are you going to do? How can I help you?" I realized how lame and useless I sounded, but I knew of no protocol for such circumstances. I could see that attractive man again in my mind's eye and found it almost impossible to believe he could be involved in something like this. I always thought I could judge people with some accuracy, but I couldn't have been more wrong.

Beth's face had not regained its color. She stared at me with some remnants of suspicion still in her expression. "You knew nothing about this? This...this... horrible note?"

"Oh, Beth, of course not. It happened exactly as I told you. I can't tell you how awful I feel. I had no idea it was anything but a favor. He seemed like such a nice guy."

"Well…sure, okay. I guess you wouldn't be here if you were involved. I'm such a basket case I can't think straight."

"The least I can do is help you out. Surely there's something I can do for you."

Beth closed her eyes and rubbed her temples with her forefingers. "I've got to get my thoughts in order. There is one thing. I usually leave my car at the motel up there by the entrance to the path. I made arrangements with them when I started this painting. But this morning I had to take it to a garage on the Trail for new brakes and some work on the engine. They dropped me off here and were going to pick me up at five. It'll be all torn down now, so even if I called them, I couldn't drive it. Could you take me home?"

"Of course I will. Don't you live with your grandmother? That's what the article said."

"That's right. Oh, Lord. I've got to get there to see if she's really gone. Can we hurry?"

"Do you want to call first to see if she answers? To make sure this isn't some kind of a sick prank?"

"Her hearing's bad. She can't hear the phone ring. It just usually goes to voice mail and I pick up the messages when I get home."

"Let's go, then. I'm parked across from the motel," I said, picking up the easel and folding stool while Beth put the letter back in the box. I followed her wordlessly as we hurried down the path toward the car. I opened up the back end of the hatchback, and we put the painting supplies and canvas on top of the groceries.

"Don't you live on Casey Key?" I asked, again recalling the newspaper article.

"Yes. Near the north end."

I retraced my route back to Tamiami Trail and headed south. Neither of us spoke as I drove as fast as I dared along the busy five-lane highway, past blocks of retail stores and restaurants, past Sarasota Square Mall and Pelican Plaza. We were finally out of the highly developed retail area of Sarasota and passing the exclusive and enormously expensive residential area, the Oaks, spread out behind tall landscaped mounds of grass that give passersby only tantalizing glimpses of the mansions behind the security gates. Quickly we went from there to the tacky few blocks of what constitutes the retail area of Osprey. Typical of the state, I thought. The old "cracker" Florida juxtaposed against the flamboyantly extravagant "new" Florida.

At last, to break the tense silence, I spoke.

"I know you must be frantic, but it really could be some kind of a cruel joke. People sometimes do unbelievable things thinking it's funny."

Beth, who'd been staring out the side window, turned toward me. "I pray you're right. But I'm terrified you're wrong."

I took my eyes off the road just long enough to glance at her. Beth was an attractive young woman; not beautiful in the Hollywood sense, but wholesome with an oval face, large brown eyes and, now that her color had returned, a peaches-and-cream complexion. Her very short hair framed her face with auburn curls. Her left hand was lying on her leg, and I put my hand on hers and gave it an encouraging squeeze.

"Have you always lived with your grandmother?" I asked.

"No, just the past few months. My parents died in a car wreck several years ago, and Grandy is all I have left. And I'm her only relative now." Her voice started to break again. She paused a moment, took a deep breath and then continued. "I lived in Virginia and visited as often as I could. But after Christmas I realized how much she was failing. Her eyesight's poor and she's getting a little confused. I knew she shouldn't be left alone. So I asked if I could come live with her, and she cried and said she'd wanted me to for a long time but didn't want to be an imposition. As if she could be an imposition." She began to cry, so I didn't ask anything more.

We'd reached Blackburn Point Road, the northern access to Casey Key which is directly south of Siesta Key. In fact, now that Midnight Pass that separated the two had silted over, much to the deep regret of boaters, at low tide one could almost wade from one island to the other. I turned right and drove down the two-lane road lined with mangroves and across the narrow rusty bridge that connects it to the mainland. This singularly unattractive bridge gives no hint of the beauty and wealth one is about to encounter. Casey Key is a unique Florida island in that it is almost completely single-home residential. There are no high-rises, no monstrous hotels, no shopping centers. Only a few small, old motels and rental places are clustered around the southern access road to the key, which leads into public Nokomis Beach. Beyond that lies North Jetty Park that includes all the southern tip of the island. The island is narrow—only one road traverses its length, with just enough room on either side of the road for a generous lot, and in places it is only a single lot wide. Large, magnificent homes occupy these sites, which in most cases were preceded by small modest homes that were torn down. Only an occasional original home can be seen, dwarfed by its newer neighbors. The entire key reminds me of a Disney version of a tropical island, with lush plants and thousands of sabal palms, all of which seem far too perfect to have sprung up naturally. But the effect is splendid nevertheless.

Beth directed me to turn north when we arrived on the key. Not far from the intersection she pointed out a driveway on the right. I pulled my car up beside an older redwood-sided home. It was an attractive V-shaped house, nowhere close to the size of the new ones we'd passed, but certainly roomy enough. It had the somewhat shabby look of a house that had weathered storms and mildew-inducing humidity over the years without a lot of maintenance and upkeep. The surrounding shrubbery had grown up, some of it embracing the house as if a very part of it, the structure becoming one with nature. It seemed appropriate for a Florida home somehow. The new houses, so pristine with their clipped hedges and sparkling paint, looked like they belonged somewhere else, certainly not the tropics.

As soon as I turned off the engine, Beth was out of the car running toward the front door. She threw it open—it was apparently unlocked—calling, "Grandy, where are you?"

I trailed after her and stepped inside where I could hear Beth still calling her grandmother's name down the hall to the left, which, I assumed, was the bedroom wing. I waited for her beside the front door, too uncomfortable to follow her through the house. I didn't want to sit down, either. I felt very strange being there, involved with someone I barely knew in such a dramatic, perhaps life-threatening situation.

The front door opened directly into a large living room with an immense stone fireplace on the wall to the right. Corner-to-corner windows on the back wall overlooked a yard allowed to go back to nature, where huge live oak trees with intertwining branches shaded myriad plants: sea grape, hibiscus that had obviously once been part of a more formal garden, palmetto and much more. The lot sloped gradually down until it met the Intracoastal Waterway. The room was paneled in a dark wood and had a soaring ceiling with exposed rugged beams. Furnished in a hodgepodge of comfortable, worn-looking furniture, it reminded me a great deal of my home in Columbus. I've always been drawn to homes that look as though they've been put together from treasured family pieces that evoke memories of past times.

I noticed a particularly threadbare chair that was turned toward the window. Beside it was a TV tray holding a partially knitted afghan, and, underneath, a large tote bag was lying on the floor, the colorful balls of yarn and several sizes of needles spilled out across the worn Oriental rug. There was something so poignant about the scene I almost burst into tears myself.

After exploring the bedrooms, Beth crossed the living room to a door beside the fireplace and went into what I later learned was the kitchen. Very shortly she returned to where I was waiting. Her face was pale again, and she seemed beyond despair. "She's not here. They've really done it! They've taken Grandy!"

"Could she be visiting a neighbor?" My mind was grasping for answers that could deny the reality of what Beth was saying.

"No. Oh, God, poor Grandy. Besides her hearing and eyesight being bad, she has arthritis, too. It's difficult for her to walk. About the only time she'll leave the house is when I take her for rides."

We both stood for a few minutes in awkward silence. Finally Beth said sadly, "Thanks so much, Emma, for bringing me home. No point in your staying here. I'll call the garage and have them deliver my car whenever it's fixed. Sorry you had to get mixed up in this."

"You are going to contact the police, aren't you?"

Her mouth set in a grim line, she shook her head. "I can't. They inferred they'd kill her if I did."

"The kidnappers don't have to know. The police will be discreet."

She closed her eyes tightly in a spasm of anguish before she responded. "I can't take that risk. I don't care what they want—I'll find some way to give it to them. Grandy's all I have left."

I could tell from the tone of her voice and the look of utter determination on her face that it was useless to argue with her, however much I disagreed. So I changed the subject to another matter. "I keep thinking about that man who gave me the note. He was probably in his fifties, tall and attractive, and his hair had quite a bit of gray. Do you remember talking to someone like that?"

Beth shook her head dejectedly. "So many people come up to look at my painting. But that description doesn't ring any bells. And no one ever talked to me about a gallery in New York. He made that all up just to get you involved."

"I've been wondering why he used me to deliver the ransom note to you. Why involve another person?"

She pondered the question for a few minutes as if she hadn't thought about it before. "I would guess they wanted to make absolutely sure I didn't call the police. If they'd left the note here, I might have overlooked it in my panic when I found Grandy missing. My first instinct would have been to call 9-1-1."

A couple of other questions were on my mind, too. Though it really was none of my business, I figured I had the right to ask since I'd been unwittingly drawn into this unbelievable situation.

"Is your grandmother wealthy?"

"Grandy's comfortably well-off, but by no stretch of the imagination would anyone call her wealthy. But anyone who lives on Casey Key is perceived to be rich.

Grandy's lived in this house for over fifty years, and back then you didn't need a lot of money to buy a place here."

"Who would know you'd be at the beach at a certain time and that your grandmother would be alone?"

Beth chewed on a fingernail as she thought about it. Then a stricken look convulsed her features. "It had to be the newspaper article. Oh, dear God, I was so thrilled to get the publicity that I never thought about any danger. But it said I could be found every day at Point of Rocks at noon, and it also mentioned that I live with Grandy on Casey Key. It gave her full name. All someone had to do was look it up in the phone book."

"Oh, Beth, please don't blame yourself. You couldn't have known this would happen."

She was quiet for a minute. Then she said, "I'll never, ever forgive myself. I was so thoughtless when I talked to that reporter. All I could think of was what was good for my future as an artist."

I put my hands on her shoulders and looked her squarely in the eye. "Beth, you've got to stop beating yourself up. That's not going to help your grandmother."

She put her arms around me and gave me a hug. As she pulled away, she brushed tears from her eyes. "You're so kind. I can't thank you enough."

"What else can I do?" I asked. "I don't want to leave you alone like this."

"Emma, I can't impose on you anymore. I'll be all right. There's nothing to be done until I hear from them again. Why don't you give me your phone number? I'll call you when I know something. Okay?"

I felt terrible leaving her like that, but I understood her need to be alone. She wouldn't want or need a virtual stranger around when she'd have to deal with the ransom demand. Their financial status was none of my business. And she probably thought that my presence could further jeopardize her grandmother. Whoever had sent the note had accomplished their goal, because she was going to proceed exactly as they told her to. She wasn't going to take even the slightest chance of putting Grandy in any more danger than she already was. I pulled out a little notepad I carried in my purse and wrote down my phone number. "Here's how you can reach me. Promise me you'll call if there is anything at all I can do."

She took my hand in both of hers. "I promise, Emma. I know this is going to work out, and I'll get Grandy safely home again."

She walked me out to the Civic, and I started to get in. "Oh, Beth, your things. We forgot all about them." I walked around and opened the back of the car. Beth picked up her canvas and art equipment, and we saw that the bags underneath had wet patches on them where the frozen food had melted.

"Look. Your groceries are ruined. Let me pay you for them"

"Don't be silly. It's no big deal. You have much more important things to worry about. Besides, I can probably save most of it."

I watched her trek sadly back to the house before I backed out of the driveway with my load of melting food and headed home. I wondered what in the world would become of Beth and her grandmother. In the space of a little over an hour, I had become a part of their lives and somehow partially responsible for the tragedy that had befallen them, even though I knew events were totally out of my control.

THREE

I HAD TO THROW OUT THE ice cream, contained in a plastic bag, which had turned to soup. But the rest of the frozen food held enough ice crystals that I stuck it in the freezer, hoping I wouldn't die from some bacteria multiplying in the thawed parts.

By the time I'd put everything away, I realized how bushed I was. The tension of the past couple of hours had taken its toll, and I felt limp and exhausted, wanting nothing more than to eat some lunch, take a nap and spend the evening with a good book. But I was supposed to go to a dinner party at Ross and Jean Jacobs's place, two doors down the hall. Although we'd had a nodding acquaintance ever since I moved into La Hacienda over a year ago, we recently became good friends, one of the neighbors who had helped me through the grieving process when Paul died. They had taken me under their wing and had been most kind to me.

They'd invited Cal Murray to the party, as well. The most positive thing in my life currently is my friendship with Cal, a retired journalist who occasionally writes freelance travel articles to keep his hand in. He makes a caring and stimulating companion. We are not lovers, just very good buddies.

I did want to see him; I knew I could share my feelings of guilt and frustration over the day's events with him, but a dinner party wasn't the place to do it.

I ate a bit and lay down to rest for a while. I awoke with a start and, when I glanced at the clock, was shocked to see it was nearly six o'clock. Dragging myself off the bed, feeling about as lively as the seaweed out on the beach, I showered and dressed in a pair of batik patio pants in blue with a white tunic top. Hardly anyone wears skirts at La Hacienda. After a lifetime of panty hose, the women here have declared their independence from miserable fashions like hose and high heels.

Cal knocked on my door at a little before seven. Bless his heart, he is always so punctual, you could almost set the atomic clock by him.

"What's up?" he asked, his gray eyes giving me one of his sassy looks. "Knowing you, I'm sure there's something going on." He was wearing a long-sleeved pale blue dress shirt unbuttoned at the neck and navy pants, and his dark hair curled slightly over the edge of his ears. The encroachment of gray at his temples makes him look like a distinguished professor. He leaned over and kissed my cheek. Another reason not to wear high heels: Cal is only a couple of inches taller than I am, though his five-foot-ten frame is nicely proportioned.

"Don't ask," I said. "At least not now. It's nothing I can discuss at a dinner party."

"Aha, I knew it. Something's afoot." Even though he was reacting jovially, I knew from experience that he cannot deal well with anything that puts me in the slightest danger. That did tend to make me consider carefully what I told him and what I withheld.

We walked to the neighbors', and Ross Jacobs answered my knock at the door of 1108.

"Emma, Cal, good to see you. Come on in." He is a large man, tall with a stocky build, with a halo of white hair and a neatly trimmed beard. He looks like a sea captain, and, indeed, he and Jean have a fairly large sailboat which they frequently sail around the Florida peninsula. When they aren't on their boat, they have a packed social calendar. These two face each day with the enthusiasm and anticipation of teenagers, though they've reached their late seventies.

Jean came out to the foyer to greet us. She is as dainty as Ross is large. I can look down at the top of her head. Her hair is dyed strawberry blond, and on her, I have to admit, it looks wonderful. I've never even used a rinse, but then people always comment on what a great job my beautician has done highlighting my hair, when in fact it's all due to Mother Nature.

She greeted us in her usual ebullient way and took my arm and walked me into the living room, Cal following behind. Several people were having an animated discussion, though I did not recognize any of them.

"I'd like you to meet Joe and Martha Schellenger. They live down on the sixth floor."

I smiled and nodded at the very elderly couple who looked like fraternal twins with their round pink faces, snow-white hair and identical glasses. Martha had a three-legged cane beside her chair, and Joe apparently had suffered a stroke. His left arm was supported by a sling and his smile was one-sided. A number of La Hacienda residents were at this stage: struggling to stay in their homes and resisting the move to assisted living or a nursing home. I admired their gutsiness.

Jean introduced us next to a younger couple sitting side by side on Jean's elegant green damask sofa. "I don't believe you've met our son, Sam, and his wife, Barb."

"Don't you live here in Sarasota?" I asked pointedly as I shook their hands. It was mean of me, but I hoped they'd get the hint. They never visited his parents, at least that I knew of. And Jean and Ross rarely talked about their son and daughter-in-law, which I always thought was strange. But I'd sensed that there was a reason for it, so I'd never inquired. After six months of seeing the Jacobses socially, this was the first time I'd laid eyes on them.

Sam, who was standing now, was nearly as big and husky as his father. "Yes, we do." He laughed, apparently not picking up on my little dig. "It's just that Barb and I both are so busy we don't get over here much. Besides, you know how hard it is to catch up with my parents."

Barbara was nearly as tall as her husband, though slender. She was dark-haired and dark-eyed in a kind of sultry, sexy way. Sam gazed at her with such obvious infatuation it was almost embarrassing. I was reminded of boys in junior high who'd mooned over the class beauties, and their inordinate joy if their interest was reciprocated. It appeared to me that Sam had never gotten past this stage.

I glanced at Cal as he shook Barbara's hand. It seemed to me his smile was a bit broader than usual, and he held her hand just a tad too long. Men!

"You know during tourist time I think it's easier and faster to drive across the state than drive across Sarasota." Barbara seemed to feel the need to explain their infrequent visits to her in-laws. "We live on the far northeast side of town, close to the insurance office where I work. And Sam has to drive up 75 to his job in Ellenton. So it takes forever to get to Siesta Key. Mom and Dad Jacobs come to our house more often than we come over here. We working folk seem to have so little time." Her voice was low and throaty and reminded me of Lauren Bacall.

Well, maybe that was a valid excuse. It wasn't as if Jean and Ross were in poor health and needing assistance. I knew others in our building who struggled with everyday tasks, whose local children rarely helped them, let alone visited. Those kids I wanted to strangle.

Another older couple was introduced next, Steve Eberhart and Elizabeth Wagstaff, both quite affable and attractive. My curiosity aroused, I began speculating about their relationship. I wondered if they were married and Elizabeth had kept her maiden name, somewhat uncommon in their age group. Or were they living together, though unmarried? Perhaps they were only dating. She had a plain gold band on her ring finger, but that could mean anything since widows often wear their wedding rings. I do so myself. The couple seemed so attentive to each other I was certain they were sweethearts or newlyweds.

I instinctively reached for Cal's hand and squeezed it. He, in turn, gave me a questioning look, and I smiled back. I couldn't tell him here how much his friendship meant to me. I'd felt such melancholy after Paul died, and Cal, along with Jean and Ross, had pulled me out of that black hole that was sucking me downward.

"Well, now that you've met everyone, I've got to check on things in the kitchen," Jean said.

During dinner the discussion was quite lively. All in all, it turned out to be a mostly pleasant evening. Even though my mind kept wandering to Beth and her grandmother, I kept forcing it back, not wanting to have the evening completely spoiled by worries over their situation. It wasn't until Jean's daughter-in-law mentioned her own grandmother, who had recently gone into a nursing home, that I was plunged totally back into the turmoil of the afternoon.

"It's an awful place," she commented. "She feels like a prisoner there. But it was the only one that had an opening when my mom was looking for a place for Grandma."

The irony of her statement hit me hard, and it was all I could do to maintain my composure after that. Though I tried very hard to keep up my end of the conversation, I couldn't get my mind off the woman who was in fact a prisoner.

I was relieved when the party finally broke up and I could go home.

Cal walked me to my door. "Are you feeling okay?" he asked. "You didn't have much to say during dessert and afterward. I was concerned about you."

This was the point where I was planning to invite him in and fill him in on at least some of the afternoon's experience. But I realized then that he would probably overreact and beg me not to get involved in any way. Chances are I wouldn't. But on the other hand, I wanted to feel free to do whatever I thought necessary to help Beth should she contact me again.

"I'm just really tired tonight for some reason. I hope you don't mind if I don't invite you in."

"I thought you had something you wanted to talk to me about."

"Not that important." I shook my head, thinking what a liar I was. "It can wait." Maybe forever, I thought to myself.

He took my hand. "Okay, then. Do you want to go out to dinner on Saturday night?"

"Sure, Cal. That would be fine."

"I'll pick you up at seven-thirty. Now, go get some rest. I expect you to be ready to go nightclubbing and dance till dawn."

"Yeah, right," I said. Cal is no more of a night owl than I am. We both need our sleep. And it isn't our age, either. We both have been morning people all our lives and tend to fade fast after ten o'clock.

He gave me a big hug. "See you Saturday."

I watched him till he got on the elevator. What a kind man, I thought.

I went straight to bed, not even bothering to hang up my clothes. As I lay there waiting for blessed sleep, my thoughts were now solely on Beth and Grandy. Why was I dwelling on them so? I wondered if it had anything to do with how much I'd always wanted a daughter. When Mark was born, I had to have a hysterectomy, and so of course I could have no more children. Not that I don't adore Mark and spoil him rotten. Always have and always will. But I'd always wished there could have been a daughter, as well. I felt that it would be a different kind of a relationship in that we could share interests and passions that are uniquely feminine, the way Mark and Paul had that special masculine tie.

Somehow I'd developed a kind of uncanny bond with Beth, even though we'd spent such a short time together. Only rarely do I experience such a strong affinity for people I meet. Perhaps sympathy for her plight had much to do with how I felt, to say nothing of the guilt I couldn't shake for my unwitting role in it. And I wondered if her powerful love and concern for her grandmother played some role in this, too. I had no grandchildren, but if I ever did, I would hope to have as strong a bond with them as Beth did with Grandy. There was a warmth and sensibility about Beth that I responded to immediately. And I couldn't help but worry about her as much as if she'd been my own daughter.

FOUR

I SLEPT RESTLESSLY. IT SEEMED as though I'd checked the clock at least every hour throughout the night. Finally at six I gave up and made myself my usual cereal, banana and coffee breakfast.

I'd planned on running errands that morning, but I didn't want to leave, just in case Beth called. I was torn. In a way I wanted to hear from her because I was anxious to know what was happening. On the other hand, I didn't want her to call because that might mean things weren't working out for her. I was on an emotional roller coaster and I couldn't seem to get off.

Finally I decided to do a washing, though I normally do that on Saturday.

I'd finished two loads when the phone rang a little before ten. It was Beth. My body went cold: it had to mean trouble.

And I was right.

"I have an enormous problem, Emma. And I didn't know who else to call."

I'd been so afraid this would happen. "What is it, Beth?"

"The kidnappers called yesterday and gave me till this afternoon at three to get the ransom together.

Grandy has a sizable bank account and a couple of CDs in both our names which cover a large part of what they want. But everything else is in her name only." Her voice became tearful. "She and I had talked a couple of times about getting me a power of attorney so I could handle her affairs if she should become ill or incapacitated. But we'd put it off for one reason or another. I was always busy with classes or work or something. And of course I selfishly wanted time to do my paintings."

I was not at all surprised at this. Paul and I had done the same thing, postponed making important financial decisions. It wasn't simply procrastination, but an unwillingness to face the obvious: we're all going to die someday. It had been a costly mistake because most of his assets were in his name alone rather than held jointly. It made it more difficult to settle his estate, and I had been virtually penniless for a short period of time.

"What am I going to do?" she continued. "I don't have much money of my own. About six hundred bucks is all."

"Oh, Beth. That's awful," I agreed.

"I thought you might know of someone who would loan me the rest of the money. Just till Grandy comes home. Then I can pay them back. She has stock she can sell. She can easily cover it."

"How much do you need?"

"Thirty-six thousand dollars. They're demanding two hundred thousand, and I've managed to put a hundred and sixty-four together."

"That's a lot." I tried to think of someone I could go

to. Obviously I couldn't go into a bank and ask for a loan to pay off kidnappers. What do you say to them? Please give me thirty-six thousand dollars for a ransom but don't tell anyone about it? For one brief second I thought of Jean and Ross. They had loads of money. But I remembered Jean saying the night before that they'd be out of town today. And although they were friends, I couldn't imagine myself asking them for that kind of money—particularly when I'd have a most difficult time explaining why I needed it. Beth was adamant about keeping this a secret from everyone for fear they'd contact the police. Cal certainly didn't have that kind of money. And I'd already decided not to tell him about Beth and Grandy, knowing he would worry himself sick over my involvement.

I realized then that there was no other way to obtain that much money except to loan her some of mine. But I had to do some soul-searching first.

"I'll see what I can come up with, Beth. Give me a little time."

"Oh, bless you. You are a lifesaver! But please don't take too long," she pleaded. "I'm running out of time and I'm so scared!"

I tried to reason with Beth once more. "If you went to the police, they'd handle all this for you. I think you are making a huge mistake by doing this on your own."

"Oh, God, no, Emma. I simply can't take the chance. I'm so petrified they'd kill her if I did. She's so helpless. When I finally got to sleep last night I had these nightmares about what they'd do to her. It was horrible." Her voice broke. "Please don't make me do that."

I sighed. "Well, let me see what I can do. I'll call you back shortly."

Paul had a life insurance policy that paid me five hundred thousand when he died. I'd invested much of it in CDs and mutual funds, but I'd kept a good chunk of it in an interest-paying money-market account until I could decide exactly what I was going to do with it. At one time I'd thought I might have to help out Mark when he'd changed jobs. As it turned out I didn't, but it felt good to have funds around for emergencies. And I'd wanted to see just where the economy was going before investing more because it seemed in such a state of flux.

I sat on the sofa staring out the window toward the Gulf. This was an extremely large sum of money I was considering loaning to Beth, whom I scarcely knew. But how could I ever live with myself if Beth's grandmother was killed because I had refused to help? Even if it turned out that Grandy couldn't pay me back the entire amount once she was released, surely it was money well spent. With Paul's generous pension and other savings and stocks in addition to the insurance money, I could afford to lend it to Beth. What could be more important than saving this woman's life? I finally decided I couldn't in good conscience turn Beth down. I dialed her number and she picked up the phone immediately.

"I'm in a position to help you out," I told her.

"Can you really?" Beth's voice registered the first

hopeful tone I had heard from her. "I...I can't tell you what this means to me. You are an absolute godsend."

"When do you have to have it?"

"They're to call back at three. They want assurance I have the money then. And they'll give me further instructions."

"I'd better hustle, then. I'll be there as soon as I can."

I dressed hurriedly and found the checkbook for my money-market account, which was held at my broker's along with various stocks that Paul had bought and my recently purchased mutual fund. That way all my dividends were rolled over into my money-market account, which also included the insurance proceeds that I hadn't yet invested, where it was available to me at any time. In the process of settling Paul's estate, I'd gotten to know the branch manager of my bank in South Gate Shopping Center so well, I was reasonably sure she'd allow me to cash a check immediately instead of having to wait a few days as was their custom for large amounts of money. Since my CDs were held there, they would suffice as collateral.

As I'd hoped, Margaret Peterson, the manager, cashed the check for me on the spot.

"You must be going on one heck of a shopping spree," she kidded me as she counted it out in five-hundred-dollar bills as Beth had specified.

"Sometimes you find you have to help the kids out these days," I replied, letting her think it was my own kid who needed the help. "They seem to have trouble making it on their own."

"Isn't that the truth. You and I would never have asked our folks for help, would we?" Margaret was probably in her sixties.

"I don't think any of our folks could afford to," I replied.

I forced a smile and left, trying to appear as cool and unruffled as possible. I didn't know why I felt so guilty doing this; after all, I wasn't doing anything illegal. But the whole situation left me feeling strange and anxious.

I arrived at Beth's house by a little after one and pulled in behind a two-door Chevy that, from its faded paint to its rusting chrome, looked to be at least fifteen years old, if not older.

Beth answered the door dressed in chino pants and a black T-shirt.

"I see you got your car back," I said as we seated ourselves on the pink couch.

"Thank God for that. And thank God for plastic. It cost more than I expected, as always. I'll be paying that off for months."

When I showed her the money, Beth burst into tears once more. "Oh, Emma, you've saved our lives. My life wouldn't be worth living if I couldn't help Grandy and get her back." She enveloped me in a huge hug, and I could feel her heart pounding in her chest. I'm sure mine was, too. This was an "adventure" that neither of us wanted to be on, but we were stuck with it.

We went to work wrapping the money in small foil bundles according to the kidnapper's instructions. Beth had already wrapped the money she'd been able to get together, and it was stashed in the bottom of two very large sailcloth carrying bags that had a Monet water lily painting on their sides, probably something she used to carry art supplies in under ordinary circumstances. The tops had flaps that folded over and closed with Velcro.

"May I wait with you till you get the call?" I asked. "I want to make sure everything's okay."

"Please do. I'm a nervous wreck, and it would help to have you here."

We passed the next hour in the backyard, where plastic patio chairs were gathered around a plastic table close to the waterway in the shade of a huge live oak. I noticed that the cabbagelike smell of the jungle growth was strong after a nighttime shower. We tried to make small talk, but as the tension mounted it grew more and more sporadic. Mostly we drank coffee while we watched the boats make their way up and down the Intracoastal. A mockingbird sang lustily nearby, but the tranquil setting did nothing to calm us. I noticed how Beth's foot jiggled and the way she gripped the arms of the chair until the veins stood out on the backs of her hands. I was beginning to feel nauseous and I knew it was nothing but nerves.

Around two-thirty the sky started to fill up with towering cumulus clouds, and a brisk breeze began to blow in from over the Gulf. Very quickly it grew ominously dark, and soon scattered drops caused us to pick up our cups and head toward the house in a jog. Before we could reach shelter, it had turned into a downpour;

we were saved from a complete drenching only by the thick canopy of leaves that the live oaks provided.

"Oh, damn," Beth complained as we stood bedraggled in the kitchen washing up the coffee mugs. The rain was pounding noisily on the roof. "I wonder if this is going to make them postpone contacting me. I am going to jump out of my skin if this goes on much longer. I can't stand this waiting."

"It seems like one of those quickie storms that come and go. It'll probably be over before three." I was trying to shore up my own hopes as much as Beth's.

Sure enough, the downpour soon fizzled out to a light sprinkle. The gloom had settled in to stay, though, and the wind still shook the branches in a frenzied kind of dance, but the worst of the rain apparently had headed east across the state.

I thought how fitting this gray day was for the occasion. The earlier sunshine had been almost ludicrous under the circumstances.

It was about two forty-five when we settled down in the living room. I wondered if Beth in her silence was thinking about her deceased parents. Tragic situations have a way of resurrecting memories of former catastrophes. Each trauma builds upon the past until either you break or you come out tougher and more able to withstand future blows. Was Beth strong enough to handle this situation? That probably would depend upon the outcome. I had a feeling that if anything happened to her grandmother, Beth might just fall apart. I prayed a silent prayer that the worst wouldn't happen.

The call came a little after three. Beth had been sitting at the rolltop desk for fifteen minutes in anticipation and picked up the phone immediately. Except for identifying herself, she said only "Yes, I have it," then listened intently for about five minutes. Finally she said, "Grandy..." urgently, but nothing more. After hanging up, she sat there silently, almost trancelike.

I walked over to her. "What did they say?"

Beth looked up at me startled, as if she'd forgotten I was there. "Oh," she said. "They let Grandy speak to me. She sounded awful. She just said, 'Hurry, Beth. Come and get me.'"

"So what are you supposed to do now?"

"I'm to drive over to Myakka State Park. They described a place where I'm to put the money. They said they'd be watching me the whole time. Then I have to drive on to a picnic area out of sight of where the money will be left, park in the lot and sit at a certain table. They'll check to see if the money is all there, and if it is, they'll drop Grandy off at my car. I'm supposed to wait fifteen minutes more before I can bring her home."

"How do you know they won't just take the money and run?" I didn't want to say they might just kill her grandmother anyway, but I'm sure she understood what I meant.

Beth stared at the floor. "Honest to God, Emma, I don't know. But what do they have to lose by letting her go? I've got to assume that they didn't let her see them so she wouldn't be able to identify them. And what do they want with an old lady? I've kept my part of the bargain by not calling the police. I've got to pray that they keep their part of the bargain, too."

"I think I should go with you. It's not safe for you to go by yourself," I insisted.

"They said I must come alone. Otherwise they won't release her. Even if you hid in the backseat, they'll have a chance to check the car at the picnic area. I have to park a ways from the picnic table."

"I hate this, Beth. I'm going to be worried sick about you."

"I don't have a choice. I have to do this their way."

She was adamant and there was no changing her mind. I helped her to carry the bags of money to her car and put them in the trunk. I hugged her and told her I was praying for her.

I backed my car out to allow Beth to get out of the driveway, then pulled back in and parked next to the house. I watched till Beth was out of sight. Although the wind still blew vigorously, causing the trees to shake off the rain that had accumulated on their leaves and creating big drops that splashed on my head and shoulders, I didn't think there'd be any more showers to interrupt the plan to rescue Grandy.

If I thought the past couple of hours were hard on the nerves, I knew these next ones would be even worse. What would happen to Beth? Would they really release Grandy? What if she could recognize her kidnappers? Maybe they wore hoods or masks or something. Lord, I hoped so. I was sure the life of an ailing old woman meant nothing to them. And if anything happened to

NANCY GOTTER GATES 47

her, Beth would never get over it. It was just too terrible to even contemplate. I wished Beth had not insisted on dealing with these people without the help of the police. But I understood how she felt: she was terrified of the consequences if she didn't do exactly as they told her.

I stretched out on the pink sofa to await Beth and Grandy, wondering how long it would take. It was probably a forty-five-minute drive or more to Myakka Park, which was on State Route 72, east of Sarasota. So, guessing that she would be at the park for at least an hour, she'd be gone a minimum of three hours.

The minutes dragged by so slowly I felt as if I were in a time warp. Each fifteen minutes seemed more like an hour. I tried to read the couple of old magazines I found in a large antique basket beside the desk, but it was impossible to concentrate on the words. I read whole sentences without comprehending them at all. Finally I gave up on them and closed my eyes, trying to summon up thoughts unrelated to Beth and Grandy, to put them out of my mind for a few minutes. But I found it impossible.

FIVE

AFTER THREE EXCRUCIATING hours of waiting for Beth I turned on the old TV set to watch the six o'clock news, hoping it might distract me.

It more than distracted; it stunned me! The news anchor announced that the body of a young woman had washed ashore at the north end of Siesta Key a little before five that afternoon. There was no identification on her, but her description—short, curly auburn hair, five foot six, slender, wearing chino pants and a black T-shirt—hit me like a physical blow to the gut. It sounded exactly like Beth. But what would Beth be doing there? What about Grandy? The anchor droned on, saying the coast guard had found an empty small boat fitted with an outboard motor a few hundred yards out and surmised she had fallen overboard and drowned. The sea was choppy and small-craft warnings had been posted. The Sarasota police were attempting to identify her.

There was no question; I had to find out who this person was. But how was I going to handle it? I'd go to the police and say I thought I might be able to identify her. If it wasn't Beth, which I prayed fervently was the case, I wouldn't have to bring up the subject of Grandy since I'd promised Beth I wouldn't interfere with her negotiations. I kept trying to tell myself that it wasn't her, that it was a terrible coincidence, but somehow my brain didn't want to believe. The thought of viewing the body filled me with absolute horror, but it had to be done.

I left the house, locking the door behind me though I had no key. I'd come back if the victim proved to be a stranger, hoping against hope that Beth and Grandy would be there.

I drove up Tamiami Trail into downtown Sarasota, slowed by the tail end of the rush hour, and found a parking space not too far from the police department on Ringling Boulevard. It's a relatively new building, a no-nonsense facade of brick with long narrow slits, instead of regular windows, that make it look like a medieval fort. Were they expecting to quell invaders who lay siege upon them with bows and arrows?

The lobby was small and dark with dirty brown carpet and brick walls, the only decoration a dimly lit cabinet featuring sports trophies. A uniformed woman sat at a small counter behind what I assumed was bulletproof glass, and I explained to her why I was there. Since the regular activities of the working day, such as paying parking fines, had ceased at five o'clock, the public area had taken on the rather unsettling and eerie emptiness that can inhabit a normally busy building after hours. Although by rights this place should be the safest in the city, I felt a sort of nameless dread as I waited while she called the Criminal Investigation Division. The fact that I was on the wrong side of the glass didn't help.

"Detective Caronis will be right out," she said pleasantly. "Why don't you wait there." She gestured toward three uncomfortable-looking plastic-and-chrome chairs lined up against the wall.

It was just a few minutes later when Caronis, wearing a conservative navy suit and subdued striped tie, came into the lobby through a small door that was the only access to the inner workings of the building.

He stopped short as he recognized me. "Mrs. Daniels? What brings you here?" he asked as he shook my hand. I'd met him the year before when a friend of mine was killed. He's a fairly tall man, around forty-five, with a surprisingly benevolent expression. His face is rather square, and his full head of dark blond hair and slightly lighter mustache give him a rakish air. The laugh lines around his mouth and eyes belie the hellish things he must see in the line of duty. He was smiling at me pleasantly. I hoped that meant he wasn't upset that I apparently was here in connection with another death.

"Hello again." I rose and shook his hand. "I came because I'm so afraid I might know the girl who drowned."

His smile disappeared and he shook his head sadly. "People refuse to pay attention to the small-craft warnings. It's such a shame. Kind of like the people who won't wear seat belts. Can't understand why they want to tempt fate. I'd like to verify who she is so we can notify next of kin."

Oh, my God. His remark made me realize I might be on the verge of opening a huge can of worms, because if the victim was Beth, her only next of kin was her grandmother. But, I told myself, Beth was probably at this very moment bringing Grandy home from Myakka Park. Surely she couldn't have been out in the Gulf in a little boat during a squall.

"Well, I hope I'm wrong, of course. But the description did sound like someone I know."

"The body's over at the hospital. I'll take you there."

Caronis led me out of the building to the adjacent parking lot, where we got into a nondescript gray unmarked car, a Ford, I guessed. I'm really inept at identifying automobiles.

We drove the few blocks to Waldemere Avenue in silence, a short trip as the rush hour seemed to have dissipated. The detective pulled into the emergency room entrance of the hospital and parked in a spot marked Emergency Room Only. I followed him reluctantly into the building just as the raucous sound of an ambulance peaked and then hiccuped to a stop as it swung under the portico just behind us. We walked briskly past a waiting room full of morose people, some in obvious pain, others talking quietly or reading magazines, down corridors and into an elevator. We went up one floor, walked through more corridors until we came to a door marked Morgue.

"Most people think of a morgue being deep in the bowels of the hospital," Caronis said. "Not so here. This is part of the Service Building, and the medical examiner is headquartered here."

I was light-headed and was sure my legs were not going to hold me up much longer. I'd never had a panic attack in my life, but I thought I was having one now. My breathing felt labored and my hands and feet were ice-cold. I'd had to identify Paul, of course, in the emergency room where they took him. But he'd looked like he was sleeping. This was different, a drowning victim. How did people look when they drowned? I really didn't want to know.

Detective Caronis was waiting by a viewing window for me, and as I hesitated, he gently took my arm in support. "Would you like to sit down for a minute?" With my open book of a face, I knew I must have looked like hell.

"I think I'd rather get it over with," I said, meaning I'd rather skip it altogether.

Caronis spoke softly to the young man in a lab coat, who was sitting at a desk in the corner of the room working on a computer. The man got up and came over to me with the detective. "You're here to identify the drowning victim?" he asked.

"I'm praying that I can't, but I'm afraid I do know her."

"If you'll wait just a moment, please." He went into the next room, and in a few minutes the curtains on the window parted and a gurney holding a draped form was on the other side of the glass. I clenched my jaw and willed myself not to faint or cry out or otherwise make a fool of myself. Caronis stood close to me; I suppose he suspected that he might have to catch me.

After a second's hesitation, the man pulled the sheet down to reveal a face. Although it was white and puffy, and her hair was matted about her head in slick tendrils like auburn seaweed, there was no doubt it was Beth.

"Oh, no!" I cried out before I realized I'd spoken. I was unprepared for the strong sense of loss I felt.

"You know her, then," Caronis said.

"It's Beth Wilkinson. I barely know her."

"All right. Let's go back to the station. You can tell me everything you know about her."

I wanted to tell him immediately about Grandy. But I knew I'd have to start at the beginning and give him all the details of the past day and a half. Whatever had happened to Grandy had probably already happened. There wasn't anything he could do till we got back to the station anyway.

We retraced our steps through the hospital corridors, down the elevator, through more corridors and out the emergency room entrance. The ambulance that had followed us in had already left.

"So have you been doing all right since I saw you last?" Caronis asked me as we drove back to the station.

"I've been fine. Believe it or not, my life has been very quiet up till now."

"Well, I'm sure this isn't the kind of excitement you want or need."

"I just can't believe this happened," I said.

We parked in the same spot we'd left at the police station and I followed Detective Caronis through the lobby, where the woman at the desk buzzed us through the door to the back. We took a small elevator to the third floor and went down the corridor to a door marked

Criminal Investigation Division. He ushered me through the wood-paneled reception area to a cubicle with six-foot-high partial walls. His desk was tidy, as it had always been before, with a framed portrait of his wife and three children, two girls and a boy, the only decoration other than his nameplate.

"Please sit down." He gestured toward the armchair next to the desk.

When I was seated, he asked me to tell him everything I knew about Beth.

"It's a long story," I replied, "even though it only goes back to yesterday. And it involves another person I'm very concerned about. Her grandmother."

"Better start at the beginning," he said.

I began with my early-morning encounter on the beach with the man who'd given me the note, and tried to think of every detail as I told my story.

"Did he give you a name?" Caronis asked, referring to the man on the beach. I had already described him.

"Just Tom. It didn't occur to me to ask his last name. I assumed she knew him."

When I got to the contents of the kidnapper's note, Caronis interrupted. "What is the grandmother's name?"

"I recall it was something Southard. Ann, maybe. Beth always referred to her as Grandy."

I explained how I had begged Beth several times to contact the police, but she would not.

Caronis shook his head. "People are extremely foolish to think they can deal with kidnappers alone. It very rarely works. But they're so intimidated by the threats, they'll do exactly as they are told. What can you tell me about the kidnap victim? Did you see a picture of her? Do you know her age? Tell me anything you can remember. We'll get an all-points bulletin out on her."

The best I could do was to describe Grandy's infirmities: poor eyesight and hearing, arthritis. I assumed she was in her seventies or eighties.

"What's the address on Casey Key? We'll have the sheriff get a search warrant for the house. That should give us more information about her."

I gave the address and told him about getting the money together, the phone call that afternoon from the kidnappers and Beth leaving for Myakka Park. "I can't understand what she was doing in a boat on the Gulf. It doesn't make sense."

"We'll do our best to unravel all of this. What I need you to do now is get together with our police artist in hopes he can get a reasonably accurate picture of the man you met on the beach. Let me take you to the conference room, and I'll put a call in for Randy. He's our artist. Luckily he happens to be on this shift today."

He guided me to a conference room at the back of the department, which was nearly filled by an oblong table surrounded by gray upholstered chairs. There were large sheets of paper taped to the paneled walls with lists of current investigations: robberies, burglaries, assaults, drug possession and dealing, murders—each had its separate sheet. He poured me a cup of strong coffee from a coffeemaker on a small table in the corner and left, saying Randy would be there shortly. As I waited

I wondered why this building was so depressing. Then
I realized it was the paneled walls, ugly shag carpeting,
the lack of any outside light. Maybe police departments
are meant to be grim, I thought, a constant reminder of
the business that goes on there.

A few minutes later a very young man dressed in
slacks, shirt and tie came in. "Hi," he said, extending his
hand to shake mine. "I'm Randy Kitsmiller. I work in
communications, but I do this when they need a suspect
drawing."

"Do you have to have art training?" I was fascinated
by this aspect of police work.

"Yeah, it helps. I graduated from Ringling School of
Art, but found pretty quick I couldn't support myself as
an artist. So I do some freelance work and this, in addition to my regular job."

We got to work, and within a half hour, Randy had
produced a good likeness of the man on the beach. I
thought I'd been very helpful and hoped the result would
aid the police in quickly apprehending him. I've tried
lately to become more aware of my surroundings, to
take in details of what I see. I've never been very obser-
vant before, but I've learned the hard way it's important
to one's safety to be vigilant.

Randy took me back out to Caronis's desk and handed
him the drawing. "Here's your perp," he said. "Thanks
for your cooperation, Mrs. Daniels."

The detective thanked me, too, and told me I was
free to go now. "If you think of anything else, call me."
He handed me his card. "You can call me at home if

I'm not here." He smiled his benevolent smile at me. "I know it's been a rough day for you. Why don't you go on home now."

"You'll let me know what's happening, won't you? I'm so worried about Beth's grandmother. I pray she's alive. But when she finds out that Beth is dead, it'll be worse than what she's already been through. If she gets home safely, I want to meet her and help her in any way I can."

"Don't worry. We'll keep you informed."

As I drove home, the tears I'd been holding back were now welling up, making it hard for me to see. I kept swiping at them with the back of my hand and thinking of Beth as she read the kidnap note and got paint on her cheek as she wiped hers away. When I crossed the north bridge to Siesta Key, the clouds had finally scattered to the east, and the sun was poised to plunge beneath the horizon. Usually I looked forward to the sunset as one of the most pleasant experiences of the day. But today the sun looked like a boil, and the sky around it seemed bruised and sore.

SIX

I STAYED UP FOR THE LATE news. All they had to say about Beth was that she'd been tentatively identified but police were trying to verify their information. No mention was made of Grandy. It occurred to me the police did not want to tip their hand if they were searching for her. At least they had not found a second body—yet.

I took a sleeping pill but woke up at three, tossed and turned fitfully until five. I put on a robe, made a pot of coffee and sat out on my balcony and watched the sky turn coral and then blue over the Gulf as the sun rose behind the condominium. Instead of enjoying the view, I was thinking how the days and nights marched inexorably on regardless of the tragedies of life. And with that thought I decided to have two cream-filled donuts for breakfast.

I thought it would be wise to stay close to home in case Detective Caronis called, although I dreaded hearing from him. My gut feeling was that it would be bad news about Grandy.

I was dressed and was cleaning out my kitchen cupboards when the phone rang at nine.

"Emma?" It wasn't Detective Caronis.

"Yes?"

"It's Cal. Is something wrong? You don't sound like yourself."

I couldn't believe I hadn't recognized his voice. I'd been obsessing so much about Grandy's fate and sure it would be the detective that I never expected to hear from anyone else.

"Oh, hi, Cal." I didn't know what else to say. Where would I begin? Did I even want to begin?

"Is this a bad time?"

"Uh, no. I was sort of expecting someone else to call."

There was a short silence. I realized that he probably thought I was being deliberately cool to him. Did he think I was waiting for another man to call? Before I could say anything, he spoke up, sounding a little defensive. "Well, I don't want to tie up the phone, then. I just wanted to see if I could pick you up earlier tomorrow night. I thought it would be fun to try out a new restaurant up at Holmes Beach, but because of the long drive we should leave about six-thirty."

"That would be fine," I said, trying to make my voice sound normal. I would straighten it all out when we were together. Perhaps by the next day I could talk about it. I just felt too emotionally unstrung to discuss it at this point. Everything was so confused right now.

"I'll see you tomorrow, then."

"Wait!" I startled myself as I shouted to keep him from hanging up. My plea seemed to have come out of nowhere, of its own volition.

"What?"

"Cal, I need someone to talk to. Are you busy this morning?" My words came tumbling out, and it was too late to retrieve them.

"I'm free as a bird. Do you want me to come there?"

"Would you?"

"I'll be there in twenty or thirty minutes."

I hung up, momentarily furious with myself. What made me do that? I know he's always a good listener and supportive even when I tend to go off half-cocked. But I didn't want to worry him, and I knew this whole situation would trouble him greatly. But surely now any danger to me was over. I needed someone to be a sounding board, to listen to my fears about Grandy and my sorrow over Beth. The Jacobses were gone, Mark was in Tampa, and besides, I certainly had no intention of telling my son how much money I'd loaned to Beth, money I probably would never see again. I had no one else to talk to but Cal.

I'd just finished stacking canned food back in the cupboard when the doorbell rang. Cal handed me a McDonald's bag when I opened the door. "Delivering your order for coffee and cinnamon rolls, ma'am." He grinned. He looked neat and attractive in his blue jeans and yellow polo shirt. His hair was still damp from the shower.

"Yum," I said and pecked him on the cheek. I wasn't about to confess I'd already had two donuts.

I put the rolls on a plate, and we carried our foam coffee cups out onto the balcony.

"I always envy you the view," he said, taking a seat in a wrought-iron chair.

"And I envy you your yard." Cal had the most gorgeous yard filled with exotic plants. "But then I wouldn't want to take care of it."

"Well, I wouldn't want to carry my groceries up in an elevator. So I guess we're even." He gave me his infectious grin and sipped his coffee. "So what gives?"

"Bear with me. It's long and complicated." And I told him the story from the beginning. His expressive face in turn registered curiosity, concern and finally horror as I told of identifying Beth.

"But you don't know what happened to her grandmother?"

"The police are looking for her and promised to keep me informed."

Cal took my hand. "My God, Emma, you've really been through hell. I'm surprised you got through that dinner the other night."

"I wanted to tell you about it then. But I was such an emotional wreck, I just couldn't talk about it. It was when Jean's daughter-in-law talked about her grandmother being a virtual prisoner in a nursing home that I almost lost it."

"Do you have any idea why Beth was in a boat out on the Gulf when you thought she'd gone to Myakka?"

"I've gone over and over it in my mind. The only idea I have is that she lied to me about Myakka Park for fear I'd call the police the minute she left. She was so paranoid about having them involved. Perhaps she was really supposed to meet them out in the Gulf. If the kidnappers were in another boat, they could make a really quick getaway."

"That doesn't sound so far-fetched to me. Maybe she was a very inexperienced boater and couldn't swim when she fell overboard. Didn't a squall line go through about that time? Or maybe they pushed her overboard. Perhaps Grandy is tied up somewhere alive and reasonably well."

"Then you don't think I'm crazy?"

"Look, anything's possible. The whole thing is bizarre."

"Bizarre things happen in Florida all the time."

"Yeah, you're right. They do."

We sat quietly again, deep into our own thoughts. I felt better having shared all this with Cal. If he thought I was stupid for getting involved, he wasn't letting on.

The phone rang and I hurried inside to answer it.

"Detective Caronis here," a male voice said.

"Did you find Grandy?" My heart was pounding at the prospect of the bad news I expected to hear.

"No, we haven't. We need to talk to you some more. Could you come to the station now?"

"Of course. I'll be right there."

I returned to the balcony, where Cal was finishing his coffee and cinnamon roll. "I've got to go to the police station."

"Any news on Beth's grandmother?"

"Apparently not."

"Well, maybe no news is good news in this case. There's still hope." He stood to go.

"I wish I really felt in my heart that was true."

He put his arm around my shoulder and gave me a hug. "You've had such a rough year. I understand your lack of optimism."

I looked up at him, startled. "The one thing I always consider myself is optimistic. If I lose that, I'm in deep trouble."

Cal looked chagrined. "I just meant these particular circumstances would knock anyone for a loop." He seemed to be groping for the right thing to say. I felt sorry for him.

"That's okay, Cal." I smiled. "Didn't mean to put you on the spot."

He shook his head and grinned back at me. "Sorry. I learned to be defensive during the divorce. Something I need to work on." Cal's wife had left him after thirty years of marriage, and the emotions from that trauma still come back to haunt him now and then.

We took the elevator down and said goodbye as we got into our respective cars. I promised to keep him informed, and he promised to help in any way he could.

As I drove toward downtown, I thought about our conversation. I was glad now that I'd decided to confide in Cal. He always has a great deal of empathy.

I told the woman at the front counter of the police station I was there at the request of Detective Caronis in CID. The lobby seemed more lively than it had the night before, with several people at the counter next to hers paying fines or inquiring about traffic tickets. When I told her I knew where his office was, she passed a visitor's badge through the slot at the counter and buzzed me through the door to the back.

The secretary in CID was the same stern-looking woman who had intimidated me the last time I saw her several months ago. It wasn't anything that she'd done, other than her seeming inability to smile, but the mere fact that she reminded me of my fourth-grade teacher who'd put the fear of God in me. Who knew her effect on me would last so long? After she rang his office, Caronis appeared almost immediately from inside the warren of cubicles, dressed in the same suit and tie he had on the day before. I suspected he'd never gone to bed. His eyes looked tired, and he wasn't as jaunty as when I'd seen him earlier.

"Come back to my desk," he said, and I followed him back to his tiny office. His desk was no longer neat but strewn with printouts and papers of various kinds. I sat again in the chair next to the desk.

He swiveled his chair around to face me, leaned it back and clasped his hands behind his head. He looked very serious. "I'm afraid I have bad news."

"Oh, my God, Grandy's dead, too." I was devastated. I'd been so afraid that would happen.

He leaned forward and put his hand on my arm. "I'm sorry, I shouldn't have put it that way. I hadn't thought how it would sound. What I'm trying to say is there is no Grandy. It was all a scam."

I was confused. "What do you mean, a scam?"

He sat straight again and tapped the arm of the chair with his right forefinger. "Your little friend Beth? It now appears she had no grandmother. That was all an elaborate hoax to part you from your money."

I felt ill. First I thought of all the emotional turmoil I'd gone through worrying whether Grandy was dead or alive. My second thought was the realization I'd just lost a large amount of money. Then I wondered how Beth, the young girl I came to admire so much, could do such a thing, and I was left with the sickening reality that she'd paid for it with her life.

"Please explain it to me," I said dully. I was determined not to break down and cry—for me, for Beth, for such a cruel and mixed-up world.

"Beth Wilkinson, formerly of Miami, was a student at the Ringling School of Art for a year before dropping out. She had recently been living in a garage apartment on Lido Key and waitressing on St. Armand's Circle. Moved out the end of March and quit her job. She has a mother and father and brother at home in Miami but no living grandparents. The house on Casey Key is owned by a couple from Pittsburgh who live there from November to March. They occasionally rent it out off-season through a local Realtor. Beth rented the house on April 1 for a month."

I was listening but I was struggling to take it all in.

"Could I get you a glass of water or a cup of coffee?" Caronis asked.

I shook my head no.

He continued. "She seems to have cooked up this

elaborate scenario to entrap you. Of course the man on the beach had to be her accomplice. We haven't yet found out who he is."

"There's no Grandy?" I asked as if I hadn't heard what he was telling me. I couldn't seem to take it all in.

"That's right, no Grandy. Only a young woman who very cleverly schemed to part you from thirty-six thousand dollars."

I was so stunned I didn't even know what questions to ask. "Why me, anyway?"

"Our theory is she, or they, figured that retirees living in such places as La Hacienda would be financially secure. They also, as we know from other scams, believed that older people tend to be more trusting and, certainly in this case, compassionate. Her accomplice might have watched you for a few days to see if you'd make a good target, or he might have just seen you come out of the condo and figured you fit their profile."

"What about the article in the paper? Was that all a lie?"

"We think her accomplice called the paper a couple of weeks ago. According to their records, a Tom Smith called and suggested she'd make a good story. Of course we haven't been able to track down any Tom Smith. Anyway, they took the bait and interviewed her. She gave them a real sob story about losing her parents and living with her grandmother on Casey Key to set this all up. That was a key element in the scheme. We think she used her real name because of people in the area who knew her and would see her picture in the paper. Apparently she thought she'd be long gone with the money before anyone figured out what happened, so it didn't matter. She probably even hoped you'd be so mortified to learn you'd been conned that you'd never report it. It wouldn't be the first time that happened."

I was speechless. I felt like such an utter fool to think I'd been drawn into the setup completely unaware. I'd heard of others who'd been duped, of course, but usually it was some transparent story of finding money on the street and wanting the pigeon to put up "good faith" money. Or guys who want to repair your driveway with leftover blacktop. I'd never in a million years fall for something like that. But I'd never heard of such an elaborate scheme as this. And Beth was so utterly convincing.

"How did you untangle all this so fast?"

"The fact she'd used her own name with you. When Randy and I were discussing the drawing he'd made with your help yesterday, I told him Beth's name, and he remembered vaguely knowing her at the Ringling School. From that we were able to reach her parents, and they flew in early this morning and positively identified her."

"Those poor people. To find out not only their daughter is dead, but was involved in something like this." I wondered how anything worse could happen to a parent.

"We're counting on tying up all the loose ends when we find her partner. We're putting the likeness Randy did on the news tonight. Maybe that will flush him out."

"You don't think he's gone to Rochester."

"He may be long gone, but I doubt very much it's Rochester, though we'll check it out. He wasn't going to tell you the truth about anything. Anyway, we've sent the picture out on the wire, so maybe we'll get lucky."

"When all this comes out in the news, you're not going to use my name, are you?" I couldn't bear the thought of having my stupidity broadcast to the world.

"No, we don't have to identify the victim. That would be victimizing you twice."

I looked down at my hands in my lap. I noticed the prominent veins on the backs of my hands, the vague imprint of age spots. I'd never felt so old; it was if I'd aged fifty years in the past two days.

"I wouldn't count on getting your money back," Detective Caronis said gently. "We think it probably went into the Gulf when Beth's boat overturned. But there's a slim possibility her accomplice has some of it. If we find him."

I said nothing, but tried to appear as stoic as possible. No sense in acting like a blubbering fool in front of Caronis.

"I don't know if it will make you feel any better to know that this kind of thing happens all the time. I've got to admit your case is the most creative one we've run into, but many have lost far more money."

"More than thirty-six thousand?"

"Oh, yes. One poor lady lost everything she had, one hundred and eighty-five thousand. Wiped out. A local mortgage broker told her if she'd give him money to invest in property, he could get her eighteen-percent interest every month. At first she gave him ten thousand to invest. When he paid her the interest, she was so impressed she invested another twenty thousand. It kept going like that until she'd given him all of it. What he was doing was making copies of deeds filed at the county building. Then he'd type her name in on a new form, cut out the docket and clerk numbers and glue them on and make a copy of that. When he bought a Florida stamp for it and had it notarized, it appeared she had an authentic deed."

"Unbelievable."

"She was destitute. We helped her make a utility payment so her electricity wouldn't be turned off. He got a four-month sentence and is supposed to pay restitution, but he'll never pay it. He'd blown all her money. White-collar crime is barely punished." Disgust was in his voice.

"That's criminal." I blushed when I realized I'd made a really dumb pun. But then I thought of the drug pushers who spent years in jail for a single sale and wondered at the gross inequity of the criminal justice system.

"I could go on and on. There are so many stories about guys who convince an elderly lady she needs her roof or driveway fixed, and then they befriend her and get access to her accounts. Or they call up and pretend to be a bank examiner and ask her to withdraw money to help them catch a crooked teller. Naturally, they disappear with the money."

"I'd never fall for something like that."

"I'm sure you wouldn't. As I say, yours was the most sophisticated scam I've ever dealt with. Anyone could have been roped in on that. At least anyone with an ounce of compassion."

"I'll never be that gullible again." I wondered if my heart was permanently hardened to all hard-luck stories from now on.

"Sorry it turned out this way for you, Mrs. Daniels. But at least there's not a dead elderly lady, too, which is what we thought we'd find at first."

I nodded. I agreed; at least there wasn't a dead "Grandy." I wondered if I could feel any worse than I felt now if that had happened. At least I wouldn't have been betrayed. But that thought brought me up short: was betrayal worse than a death? My God, what had they done to me that such a thought could even cross my mind!

SEVEN

I SPENT A COUPLE OF HOURS sitting on my balcony staring out at the Gulf. I had to get a grip on myself. So I lost thirty-six thousand dollars. It wasn't as if it was everything I had, like that poor woman Detective Caronis told me about. In fact, it wouldn't make a huge dent in my lifestyle. But I wondered what Paul would have thought. He was probably spinning in his grave. Of the two of us, Paul worried more about money and had been more conservative in the spending of it. It wasn't that I threw money around. Not by a darn sight. I'd always treated money with respect, but not veneration. Paul hadn't worshiped money, but to him it represented many long years of hard work. He was right to feel proud of his financial success. It hurt me more to think I'd failed as custodian of his legacy than to mourn the actual loss of funds.

I skipped lunch altogether; the nauseous feeling that overcame me at the police station lasted well into the afternoon, but by six o'clock my stomach was growling. Appetite wins out over most traumas with me. I made a turkey sandwich and sat down in front of the TV to hear the local news. I'd debated quite a while as to whether or not I wanted to watch it, but finally decided I was going to have to face the news sooner or later. It would be in the papers, too, and would probably continue until the man was found.

The local anchor related the bare bones of the story: the drowned woman found on Siesta Key the day before had been identified as Beth Wilkinson, a local resident, and she'd been implicated in a complex fraud scheme in which an elderly woman was bilked out of a large sum of money. I bristled at the "elderly" bit—fifty-eight wasn't elderly in my book—but at least they didn't give my name. They probably thought everyone who lived at La Hacienda was old. The scam was not spelled out, but I figured the details would come out eventually. The police probably refused to elaborate until Tom was caught. The story ended with the showing of the suspect sketch of Beth's accomplice.

My phone rang the moment the anchor turned to another story.

"It's Cal." He sounded subdued.

"You were watching the news."

"What a shocker. Need someone to talk to?"

"I appreciate it, Cal. Right now I think I need to sort through things for myself. By tomorrow when we go out to dinner, I'll probably be ready for a shoulder to cry on."

"I understand. And I'm glad you still want to go."

"Can't stop living."

"Atta girl."

I took a sleeping pill and went to bed early that night. Even though I'd told Cal I wanted to think about it, I really didn't. I just wanted it to all go away. But I woke up feeling slightly better the next morning. I thought a walk on the beach would be a good stress reliever. After donning shorts and a tee and my walking shoes, I started off before I realized I was heading toward Point of Rocks. I nearly turned around but then decided I should continue on. Maybe visiting the place where it all began would help exorcize a few demons. Besides, if I was going to continue to live here, I couldn't avoid that area of the beach forever.

It took me twenty minutes to reach Point of Rocks. I sat on the ledge and thought about the day I took the note to Beth. She'd been one hell of a good actress. I'd been completely taken in by her tears and the dramatic story of "Grandy." How could she have been so slick, so believable? I'd never in my life been so wrong about anyone.

I was unlocking my door after returning home when Jean Jacobs came out of her condo. "Emma! I was just coming over to see you."

"Well, come on in, then. How about a cup of coffee? Was just going to make another pot." Company would be good now. I needed to think about something else.

"Love it."

We chatted as I measured out the coffee. Ross and Jean had returned from their overnight trip late the day before.

"Where'd you guys go? Did you take the boat?"

"No, they predicted bad weather. So we drove down to Marco Island. Ross wanted to play in a golf tournament there, and he actually talked the kids into taking a day off work. So while the men golfed, Barbara and I shopped. It's so seldom we get to do anything with them."

We took our coffee cups into the living room and sat on the sofa.

"I just wondered if you'd seen this morning's paper," Jean said.

"No, haven't got around to it yet. Thought I'd go walking on the beach before it got too hot."

"Maybe you already know about it. Since we were gone, this was the first I'd read about the young girl drowning and her body washing up on Siesta Key."

So much for getting my mind off the subject of Beth. "Yes, I heard that."

"They're saying she was involved in some kind of major scam."

I could only nod my head and try not to let my emotions show. How could I admit to Jean I'd been the one she'd fleeced? I was far too embarrassed to let her know I'd been taken in by the young woman.

"I knew her." Jean sounded distraught. "It's been a month or so since I've seen her, and I didn't know her well. But I can't believe what they're saying about her."

"You knew her! How?"

"Have you been to that French restaurant, Celine's, on St. Armand's? It's one of our favorites, and we eat there fairly often. We got acquainted with her when she waited on us. She and Ross used to tease each other a lot. We'd make a point of sitting at one of her tables if we could. She was a darling girl."

"How awful, Jean. You didn't have a clue? About her being capable of doing something like this, I mean."

"Oh, God, no. She was one of those kids you'd like to take home with you. Or have as your daughter-in-law, if you know what I mean." She gave me a meaningful look.

"Uh...no. I'm not sure what you're driving at."

Jean looked distressed. "I shouldn't have said that. I'm so upset I'm running my mouth when I shouldn't. It's just that Barb and I are on different planets, I guess. But Sam is wild about her and that's the important thing."

You, too? I wondered. Why does this mother-in-law/daughter-in-law relationship so often seem to be such a difficult one? My ex-daughter-in-law, Cindy, and I have had a complex relationship. While she was married to Mark, we could barely tolerate each other. When she left him for another man, I despised her for how she had hurt him. But several months ago, circumstances changed when Cindy came to Sarasota. She literally saved my life, and it's difficult to hold a grudge when you owe someone a debt like that. But I'll have to say, she still complicates Mark's life. And of course, that always colors my feelings toward her.

"But, anyway, back to Beth," Jean continued. "The girl who drowned. She was so warm and friendly."

Probably practicing her "warm and friendly" manner so she could rope me in, I thought.

"In fact, there was even an article about her in the

paper recently. About a painting she was doing of Crescent Beach. Did you see it?"

"Oh, yes, I do remember that." I pretended I'd just recalled it. "She must have been quite talented."

"We hadn't realized what an accomplished artist she was. After that article, we wished we'd bought a picture from her. But by then she was no longer working at Celine's. And we didn't know how to get in touch with her."

You could have looked up her grandmother in the phone book like Beth tried to convince me the kidnappers had, I thought. But I said, "That's really sad." Indeed it was. Sadder than Jean would ever know.

Jean finally left to run errands. I mulled over the coincidence that my neighbor knew Beth. The more I thought about it, the more it made some kind of sense. Since Jean and Ross ate at Celine's fairly often, and it was quite a pricey restaurant, Beth would have realized they had plenty of money. And their dress and general demeanor spoke of wealth, too. They'd no doubt mentioned they lived at La Hacienda, and she'd deduced everyone who lived here was rich. That could explain how I became her target.

The telephone startled me out of my reverie.

"This is Detective Jarman in CID. I wanted to bring you up to date on the Wilkinson case."

"Oh. Where's Detective Caronis?"

"He's off for the weekend. He'll be back Monday. Anyway, Miss Wilkinson's accomplice has turned himself in. His name is Kirk Justice. How's that for irony?"

"Did the police sketch have anything to do with it?"

"Yeah. Saw himself on TV. Knew he was in trouble, so he came in this morning."

"So what did he say?"

"He had no idea it was a scam."

"Oh, sure, yeah." I couldn't help the sarcasm in my voice.

"I know it sounds phony, but a lie detector test backs him up. He'd worked at Celine's with Miss Wilkinson, and they became casual friends. Recently she asked if he would help her play a little joke on someone, sort of a belated April Fools' joke. You gotta understand this guy is really gullible. I'd say his IQ is a little on the shaky side. She asked him to have breakfast with her on Wednesday, the day he gave you the note. They ate on the patio of the restaurant in the building next to yours. She seemed to be watching the beach while they ate. Finally she gave him the envelope and told him what he was supposed to say and pointed you out."

"Do you think she was specifically looking for me?"

"He couldn't say. In hindsight, knowing what she'd done, he thinks maybe she was just looking for someone coming out of the nearby high-rises. Since there were few people on the beach that early, she might have picked you for no other reason than you were there."

"Why would he agree to do a thing like that?"

"She told him some cockamamie story that her long-dead mother had been a close friend of yours back in college. She wanted to meet you and give you the painting she was working on in honor of that friendship. She knew where you lived and found out what you looked like. But she wanted it to be a big surprise, so she'd worked out this tale about the art gallery to get you down to Point of Rocks to meet her."

"Good God, what an imagination. And he bought into it?"

"Hook, line and sinker, it seems. As I said, a very gullible guy. He sort of knocks about, takes odd jobs, lives kind of a carefree existence. He impressed me as someone who wants so desperately to be liked he'd do almost anything he's asked. He does have an airtight alibi for yesterday afternoon when she drowned. Claims he didn't make the phone call, and the lie detector backs him up on that, too. So she must have conned another friend into doing that."

"She sure went to great lengths to set me up."

"True. But the payoff was worth it...until she died."

The irony of it. I lost my money; she lost her life. For what? "Do you have any better idea what she was doing in a boat?"

"Only theories. We think she was planning to go north along the coast until she could go ashore safely, probably under cover of darkness. That way she wouldn't leave any traces like she would if she drove her car. People are bound to see you on the highways."

"The whole thing's just incredible."

"Yeah." He sighed. "Even as jaded as we are, this particular case was pretty extraordinary."

EIGHT

By MIDAFTERNOON I FELT I had to get out of the house. When Paul was alive, we'd always share our day's events with each other at the dinner table. We'd celebrate each other's accomplishments, console each other when things went wrong and work out solutions to problems. I'm not saying I told him every single thing, but close to it. It wasn't until he was gone that I appreciated how much these conversations meant to me. He didn't run my life, though I know now I depended on him more than I should have, but I found comfort in the knowledge that someone understood me, knew me pretty thoroughly inside and out. Now my home serves as a refuge most of the time. But when I desperately need to share something with him and can't, its emptiness taunts rather than soothes me.

Lacking a more creative idea, I decided to take a drive, just mosey around for a while before time to get ready to go out with Cal. Without consciously heading there, I found myself driving south on Tamiami Trail past Sarasota Square Mall. Before I knew it, I'd come up to the intersection of Blackburn Point Road. What the heck. As long as I was this close, I felt compelled to drive by the house that Beth had called Grandy's, the site of my undoing.

When I got to Casey Key I turned north, intending only to drive a little way past the house, turn around and leave. But when I got to the driveway, I turned in instead. It was obvious no one was there. The owners had probably just found out that their tenant had died. It's difficult to rent out homes or condos out-of-season in Florida; the supply greatly exceeds the demand since a large number of owners go north, particularly in the high-rent areas. And after the owners found out what their house had been used for, they might never want to rent again.

I got out of the car and walked around to the back-yard. The large windows on the back of the house afforded an unimpeded view inside. The living room looked the same as it had before, except the half-knitted afghan and the knitting bag with needles were gone. I wondered if the police had taken them as evidence, though I couldn't see how much help it would be. The kitchen looked the same, too. I could see the coffee cups that we'd used that day hanging on hooks under the cupboard where I'd put them.

I walked down to the table and chairs where we'd sat waiting for the "kidnappers" to call. Beth had seemed so strained and jumpy that day. I'd thought she was upset about her grandmother. Maybe she hadn't been acting but was nervous over the outcome of her scam, as well she should have been. I sat down in a chair and watched boats on the Intracoastal for a few minutes. God, what a waste, I thought. She was so talented and had so much to live for. I wondered whatever happened to her painting.

I looked at my watch and realized I needed to get home if I was going to be ready when Cal came. As I walked around the side of the house, I noticed a folded piece of paper under an overgrown bush. The growth was so dense that I ordinarily would not have seen it. But a chipmunk was running across the lawn, and as I watched him disappear into the shrubbery, I saw the corner of the paper reflecting a ray of light that had managed to penetrate the canopy of live oak limbs.

I picked up the paper and unfolded it. Written in pencil was a telephone number—no name, no area code, so I assumed it was local. I stuck it in my pocket, got in my car and drove directly home.

I thought about the telephone number all during the drive. Who could it be for? I knew my curiosity was probably misplaced; it was undoubtedly something innocuous like a hairdresser's number or the local fish market. I wondered if it was for the garage that had worked on her car and then felt my face flush in embarrassment when I realized what I should have known all along—her car hadn't been worked on. That was just a ploy to get me to drive her to Casey Key.

By the time I got home, I'd gone through a dozen possibilities, the most plausible of which was Kirk Justice, Beth's accomplice. I looked him up in the phone directory, but the only listing for K. Justice gave a completely different number.

One way to find out whose number it was was to

dial it, though I wondered what I would say if someone answered. I didn't need to worry. Instead of a human voice, there was a terse automated recording saying, "Please leave your message," nothing more.

I called directory assistance.

"I wrote down someone's number a long time ago," I told the operator, "but I can't remember whose phone it was. Can you help me with that?"

"Sorry," she replied. "We can only give out numbers for names, not the other way around."

Since I didn't have a computer, there seemed to be only one other thing I could do. I called the reference desk at the library and asked them to look it up in the city crisscross directory. "It's not there," the reference librarian said after a five-minute pause to look it up. "It must be unlisted. Sorry."

Obviously I was getting nowhere, and it was getting late. I dressed hurriedly in a simple burgundy A-line dress I'd had for years. I was ready just in time when Cal rang my doorbell looking snazzy in a navy sport coat and gray slacks. He was wearing one of his attention-getting ties, paisley-with-mums. So out of fashion, but so Cal. Maybe that's what I loved about him; in many ways he was a free spirit.

We drove to the north bridge, took Orange Street to 41 and drove across John Ringling Boulevard to Lido Key, which we had to cross to get to Longboat. I felt a little queasy knowing Beth had lived and worked there. At St. Armand's Circle, one of the more exclusive shopping areas in Sarasota, I saw the green awning with the name Celine's written in a discreet script. A small restaurant, it had a glowing reputation and a menu that was out of my price range. I'd never eaten there since neither Paul nor I wanted to blow a hundred bucks for dinner. Nor could Cal afford to go there, either.

I pointed it out to Cal as we drove past. "That's where Beth worked."

"That place is too rich for my blood."

"Jean told me this morning that she and Ross knew Beth. She used to wait on them. That's always been one of their favorite restaurants. They liked her so much they made a point of asking for her table."

Cal turned to me in surprise. "No kidding. What a coincidence. Do you think there's some connection there?"

I told him my theory of how I was selected, and described my meeting with Detective Caronis and the phone call from Detective Jarman. By the time I'd finished, we'd driven the length of Longboat Key with its luxury high-rises and were going over the bridge to Anna Maria Island and Holmes Beach.

I'm always amused by the contrast between Longboat Key and Anna Maria Island. Longboat's growth has been so carefully controlled, its zoning so strict in all but the northern tip, that it's the epitome of elegant, manicured living on the west coast of Florida. The building on Anna Maria on the other hand has been unrestrained, at least in its early days, the result of which is strips of tacky retail areas alternating with often down-at-the-heels beach cottages, particularly on the southern end of the island. In recent years, some of the tackier places have been torn down and nicer ones erected in their places. Beach property is always in demand. But there is still enough left of its early unbridled development that it serves as an antidote to the air of stuffiness that Longboat Key exudes.

We finally arrived at the restaurant, tucked away on a back street near the north end of the island which is Holmes Beach. The Hideaway has a casual, fishing-village decor with nets and lanterns and checkered tablecloths. It is neither flashy nor original, but has a comfortable, relaxed feel.

After we were seated at a table next to the window wall overlooking a rocky beach and the Gulf, I ordered a chardonnay and Cal a draft Mexican beer. The sun was on the horizon in a cloudless sky, casting a pink glow over the water.

"Well," said Cal, holding up his beer, "I drink to a better week next week. It's a cliché maybe, but I think that time does heal. It probably won't get your money back. But like anything else, only time can give you perspective on what happened." Then he grinned. "You see how great I am at spouting platitudes. Had it happened to me, I'd probably still be pissed off ten years from now."

I played with my glass of wine, twisting it this way and that on the tablecloth in front of me, watching the circular impressions fade as I moved it. "I guess what bothers me most is that I so misjudged Beth."

"Apparently you weren't alone. You say the Jacobses were very fond of her."

"Do you think she could have been that good an actress? I mean not just with me but with the Jacobses, too? It would be hard to fake it over a long period of time."

"I suppose it's possible. But like you say, not probable."

"She'd never been in trouble before, at least she had no record. What would make a nice girl do such a thing?"

"She must have had a compelling reason. Maybe if she hadn't died, you might eventually have found the answer."

I nodded sadly. I'd never know the why of it, and that would continue to haunt me.

"Do you know what I did this afternoon?" I asked Cal.

"How many guesses do I get?"

I laughed. "Sorry, dumb question. I drove down to the house on Casey Key that was supposed to be where Beth and Grandy lived."

Cal frowned slightly. "Was that wise?"

"Well, Beth's dead and her accomplice in jail. What could it hurt?"

"I mean aren't you rubbing salt in your own wounds?"

"Oh, probably," I admitted. "I hardly realized I was going there till I found myself at Blackburn Point. Anyway, I walked around to the backyard, and on my way back to the car I found a piece of paper half-hidden under the bush with a telephone number."

"Whose number?"

I sighed. "Wish I knew." I told him about my attempts to find out.

Cal was rubbing his chin, looking thoughtful. "It's probably not connected in any way. Maybe it blew in from the neighbor's yard."

"Oh, you're right. I'm being silly."

He reached over and put his hand on mine, giving it an affectionate squeeze. "Silly you're not."

"You're sweet, Cal."

We ordered dinner, crab cakes for me, sea bass for Cal. It was fixed simply, with mixed stir-fry vegetables and warm homemade bread, and everything was delicious. Cal even talked me into a piece of Key lime pie.

On the way home I was determined to change the subject and we chatted about other things. When we got to my door, I invited him in for coffee.

"I'll take a rain check on that. You're looking very tired tonight, Emma. I'd be willing to bet you haven't had much sleep lately."

I was grateful he was so astute.

"Why not really kick back tomorrow and relax," he said. "I think you need it. I'll give you a call next week."

He kissed me lightly on the cheek before he left.

NINE

THE NEXT FEW DAYS I TRIED to keep as busy as possible. In spite of Cal telling me to kick back, I found activity was the best way to keep my mind off things I didn't want to think about. There's always much to do in Sarasota; it deserves its reputation as the cultural center of Florida. I went to a Sunday afternoon concert at the lavender-painted Van Wezel, known fondly as the "Purple People Seater," spent Monday afternoon at an arts-and-crafts show at South Gate Shopping Center, toured the orchid hothouse and hibiscus display at Selby Gardens and finally got to the library, where I checked out an armful of books.

In spite of all my frantic running around, thoughts of Beth kept haunting me. It was true I knew her for only a short while. But we'd spent several hours together those couple of days, and I'd been completely taken in by her story of Grandy and her seemingly authentic grief. What led her to concoct such an amazingly credible hoax? Of course, thirty-six thousand dollars is a lot of money. But I found it almost impossible to believe that the girl I'd gotten to know could have been such a greedy, amoral person that money was her only motive. There had to be another, more compelling reason for her behavior.

On Wednesday I couldn't find much in the refrigerator to make some lunch, so I decided to treat myself by going out. I was on my way to a favorite place in Siesta Village when I got a sudden impulse to eat at Celine's. Their lunchtime prices couldn't be too outrageous.

It was not easy to find a parking place. St. Armand's Circle is always popular and busy, but I finally found one on a side street a block and a half away. It was another beautiful day; the wind blew in lightly off the Gulf, the gulls were chattering noisily in the vicinity of the beach a couple of blocks away and the sweet perfume from the tropical trees and flowers commingled with the tantalizing odors of baking bread from a nearby bake shop.

I stepped inside to the dark coolness of Celine's and found that while it was busy, there was no line of people waiting to be seated. During the height of tourist season, it sometimes becomes almost impossible to eat out without a very long wait.

The interior was simple but elegant with a casual country French ambience. Everything was blue and white, from the soft blue walls and pure white tablecloths to the checkered seat pads tied with bows to the chair backs. A pine armoire filled with majolica plates stood against the rear wall framed by prints of cheery country scenes along with a couple of antique street signs in French. And there were bouquets of real flowers everywhere.

A young woman in a white blouse, black skirt and frilly apron waited on me. I ordered a seafood salad.

When the waitress brought my lunch, I asked, "Have you got just a minute?"

She quickly assessed the tables on either side of me and said, "Well…just a sec, I guess."

"I'm Emma Daniels. And what's your name?"

"Marta Martinez." She gave me a guarded look, probably wondering what mischief I was up to.

"Did you happen to know Beth Wilkinson who worked here?"

Marta said nothing for a moment, her mouth set in a thin, hard line. "Suppose I did?"

"I knew her…not real well…but well enough that I was shocked by what I read about her in the paper. I wondered if I could meet you after work and talk to you about her."

Marta looked at me suspiciously. "I can't tell you anything much."

"Look," I said, realizing Marta probably thought I had a personal agenda, which of course I did. I decided to play it very innocently. "I was just so stunned when I heard she was involved in a scam, I couldn't believe it. It seemed totally out of character. I'm just trying to make some kind of sense out of this tragedy. I'm not here in any kind of official capacity. This is just for my own benefit, to come to terms with my shock over this."

"Well…I guess I could talk to you a little bit. I don't know much…really. I'm off work at four." She said this very grudgingly.

"That would be wonderful. Could I meet you at that bench out in front of the restaurant?"

"Sure. Okay. Got to go now." And Marta hurried off to the kitchen.

I wondered if I was being ridiculous. I thought maybe I ought to go get a job instead of having so much time to dwell on things. Paul always said I was the most single-minded person he ever knew. Once I had something on my mind, I'd never let go until I'd driven both of us round the bend.

RATHER THAN DRIVE ALL the way home and back again, I spent the next two and a half hours "doing" St. Armand's Circle. I don't like to shop much and had been here only twice with out-of-town visitors. I went around the circle, wandering aimlessly through shops, not really seeing what was there. My mind was preoccupied with other things. By three-thirty I'd had my fill and sat on the designated bench to wait for Marta.

About four-fifteen Marta finally sat down beside me. She no longer had on her apron but still wore the dark skirt and white blouse. Although Hispanic, she had no trace of an accent. She was unusually attractive with olive skin and dark eyes and long black hair that she wore in a braid down her back. I wondered if the waitresses were hired for their pulchritude. All the ones I'd seen at Celine's were remarkably pretty.

"I really appreciate this," I told her.

"What do you want to know?" Marta still sounded wary.

"How well did you know Beth?"

"We'd both worked here about six months, but we

weren't real close. I mean we didn't hang around together after work or anything like that."

"How did she impress you? Were you surprised when you read about what she did?"

"Totally shocked. Beth was always honest. She once followed a customer outside when she found that two fifty-dollar bills had stuck together and he hadn't realized it. And she really related to the customers, you know. She was very outgoing." Marta was beginning to relax now.

"Do you know anything about her background? Her family?"

"Not really. I knew she'd gone to Ringling. She said she'd run out of money and had to drop out for a while. She'd planned to go back sometime."

"Her family wouldn't help her with tuition? Are they too poor?"

"She didn't talk about her family. I thought there was a lot of resentment there, but I don't know why. She was a little bit mysterious, you know? Great girl, but didn't say much about her personal life." She laughed. "Not like some who can't wait to tell you all about their sex lives, their money troubles, their rotten boyfriends and their hopeless families. I guess Beth had more class."

"Do you know if she had any close friends she might have confided in?"

"If she did, it was probably at school. She really loved Ringling and was anxious to go back. She did mention several times a teacher she especially liked. Let's see... his name sounded Polish. Something like Sosetack. To tell you the truth I kind of wondered just what kind of relationship they had." She raised her eyebrows and cocked her head with a knowing smile.

I found a little address book in my purse and wrote down the name, spelling it like it sounded. "That helps. Anything else?"

Marta shrugged. "Mmm…can't think of anything."

She didn't seem to be holding anything back. I thanked her and walked back to where I'd parked my car. Driving home I decided to find the teacher she'd mentioned. Did Beth carry out this elaborate scheme for art school tuition? It seemed clear she wanted to go back, but would she go to such lengths if she was as honest as Marta claimed? Why couldn't she get a scholarship of some kind? And what was her relationship to this Sosetack guy?

THE NEXT MORNING I DROVE to the Ringling School of Art, housed in a cluster of Spanish-style buildings at Martin Luther King Way and Tamiami Trail. I parked my car on a side street and looked for the Administration Building, which was on the north side of Martin Luther King.

Inside, a grandmotherly-looking woman was seated at an information desk.

"I'm looking for a teacher by the name of Sosetack or something like that," I told her, shrugging to indicate I probably didn't have it right.

"Emile Szostak," she replied, spelling out his last name for me. "Let me look up his schedule." She thumbed through a well-worn directory. "Let's see—" she looked at her Timex "—it's about ten twenty-five. He has a life painting class in session right now, but it should be over at eleven. If you want to go to the Idelson Studio at eleven, you can probably catch him. He's free till two." She pulled out a map of the campus and showed me where to go.

I strolled around campus just to get a feel for it. Handsome pink stucco buildings with red tile roofs are set off by manicured lawns with enough live oaks and palm trees to afford patches of shade. Although many of the buildings seem to be fairly new, there's an aura of old Florida about the school that is most appealing.

I sat for a while at a round concrete table set in the lawn under a huge bottlebrush tree. The air was hot and heavy already, and I knew my car, which was parked in the sun, would be worse than a sauna. A few minutes before eleven I entered the studio, a large room crammed with easels, each featuring a different version of a comely nude lying on her side. She'd obviously been posing on a small drape-covered stage in the center of the room. The shutters on a bank of windows across one wall had been discreetly closed so that the light in the room was subdued. The few students left were putting away their paints or cleaning their brushes, while the model, now dressed in a white terry robe, was talking to a tall middle-aged man with a mustache. I assumed he was Szostak.

As soon as the model left the room, I approached him. His long, thin face, badly pitted by some long-ago acne, was partially concealed by large tinted glasses. A long, limp ponytail, gold loop earring and a dingy T-shirt that said Save the NEA and was streaked with paint struck me as the classic caricature of an art teacher. His khaki pants appeared to have been slept in.

"Mr. Szostak?" I said, wondering whether I should address him as "Professor" or "Mister" or "Emile."

"Yes?" His voice was surprisingly deep and rich.

"I'm Emma Daniels. I was wondering if I could talk to you about Beth Wilkinson."

Szostak pulled off his glasses and pinched the top of his nose as though the glasses were hurting him, though I suspected the pain was more psychic than physical. He closed his eyes in obvious sorrow and was quiet for a couple of minutes, as though trying to contain his emotions. Finally he put his glasses back on carefully, one ear at a time. "I'm so glad you came. I need to talk to someone about her. And please call me Emile."

Since it was his lunch hour, I drove him to a small sandwich place in a strip shopping center a few blocks north on the Trail, and we ordered a BLT for me and a vegetarian sandwich for Szostak along with cold drinks.

"So what is your connection to Beth?" he asked as we waited in a booth for our order to be filled.

"I met her on the beach. You probably saw the article where she was painting down at Point of Rocks on Siesta Key. I live in a condo not too far away."

"Oh, yes. Beth has been in the paper a lot recently. How I wish that first article had been the last."

"Well, that's what I wanted to know. What you

thought about Beth. What kind of person she was. I hadn't known her long, but she was one of those people you kind of instantly bond with. I couldn't square my impression of her with what the paper said she had done. It's as though I can never trust my instincts about people again."

"Beth was one of those students you instantly relate to. She had a lot of talent, but it went beyond that. She had an almost charismatic personality, as you must know. Once you'd met her, you were her friend. She was popular with both students and faculty."

Although he hadn't specifically said so, I was convinced Emile was in love or something close to it with Beth. He spoke with such affection it was hard to believe he thought of her as just another student.

"I understand she loved Ringling. Why did she drop out?"

"Lack of money. She'd had some part-time jobs, but they weren't enough. Tuition is high, and classes take up a lot of hours, so she didn't have much time to work."

"Wouldn't her family pay for school? Do you know anything about that?"

"She used to confide in me about them. Her parents wanted her to be a teacher or secretary or something traditional. They refused to pay her tuition here. Apparently they're extremely conservative people, belong to some fundamentalist church. They thought being an artist was frivolous. And they thought a lot of modern art was inspired by the devil. In fact, they've actively campaigned against the NEA."

"That must have been tough on Beth."

"Oh, God, it was. I guess they had some dandy fights over freedom of expression."

"Were her paintings controversial? The one she was doing on the beach was certainly innocuous."

"As a matter of fact they were all conservative. She was all for the right to explore controversial subjects, but her own work was very mainstream. I don't think she could ever completely overcome her upbringing. She painted Florida scenery mostly."

"Why couldn't she get a scholarship? Wasn't she talented enough?"

"Oh, yes, she had loads of talent. Trouble was she was white and came from an economically well-off family. She wasn't eligible for a minority scholarship and couldn't get one based on need. The government guidelines don't cover those students whose parents refuse to pick up the tab. And she wouldn't be considered an 'independent' adult till she was twenty-four. She did pick up a small scholarship based on her ability, but it was nowhere near enough to pay full tuition."

Our number was called at the counter and Szostak brought back the tray with our sandwiches and drinks.

We ate without speaking for a few minutes while I thought of other questions to ask.

Finally I said, "What kind of part-time jobs did she have?"

"Flipping hamburgers for one. And the last semester she was in school, she was a model for the life drawing class."

"A nude model?"

"Of course."

"And what did her parents think of that?"

"I'm quite sure she never told them. From what she said to me, they'd have been outraged. But here at the school no one thinks anything about it. You can't learn to paint bodies by painting statues. You have to see how the muscles and tendons and bones work in different poses. You have to know what is under the skin to paint the human form properly. Beth had a lovely body and she was not ashamed of it."

Did Szostak lust after that lovely body? I wondered. Sure that he would not answer such a question had I the nerve to inquire, I asked instead, "Did she have any close friends among the students?"

He fingered his earring in thought. "She was well liked as I told you, but she didn't have time to make close friends. At least none that I was aware of." He took the final bite of his sandwich.

I, of course, was wondering if she was spending her time with Emile. That could keep her busy.

"So what do you think?" I asked him.

"About Beth?"

I nodded.

"That's the damn trouble. I don't know what to think. I keep trying to figure out what went so wrong in her life that she would get mixed up in some crazy scheme. It's really bugging the hell out of me."

"Do you think she would have done it for tuition money?"

"It doesn't seem like something Beth would do. But, on the other hand, what else would she need money for?"

"Maybe she was tired of living hand to mouth. Maybe she wanted nice clothes and all the gadgets everyone else craves these days."

He shook his head sadly. "Whatever. It just doesn't jibe with Beth's personality. She was never much for material things."

"Is there anyone else at the school I could talk to about her?"

"Not that I know of. I'm pretty sure I knew her as well as any faculty member because she liked to hang around after class and talk with me. I sometimes thought I served as kind of a substitute parent since her relationship with her folks was so strained."

We finished our drinks and I took him back to the school. As he got out of the car, he leaned down and said, "If you ever do figure out what happened, let me know, will you?"

"Sure," I replied.

He seemed inordinately fond of her. Was he really like a "substitute parent" to her, or was there much more to it than that? Maybe I was reading too much into all this.

I stuck my head out the car window and called after him. "Emile!"

He turned around and came back. "Yes?"

"Why don't you give me your phone number. That way I can call you if I come up with anything."

"Good idea."

I pulled out my little notebook. "Fire away."

He told me his phone number and I recorded it. It didn't sound familiar, but I wasn't sure. After he left, I pulled the slip I'd found on Casey Key out of my wallet and compared the numbers. No match at all.

TEN

THAT EVENING I ALMOST decided to give it all up. It seemed as if the process of learning anything about Beth would be as difficult as counting the grains of sand on Siesta Beach. So I'd never know what her motive was. So what? My money was gone. Delving into her psyche wasn't going to change that.

But by 3:00 a.m. my subconscious took over and woke me up, letting me spend the hours till dawn tossing and turning, my brain percolating with unanswerable questions.

By 5:00 a.m. I was up having coffee. Since everything I'd heard to this point was that Beth was an upstanding citizen, honest and caring, somehow I had to prove she wasn't the cynical rip-off artist as portrayed by the police. Of course, all the evidence so far was on their side, but there had to be more to it, something that none of us knew yet. It dawned on me, as I sat on my balcony watching the sky brighten slowly and turn the sea from black to a soft gray-green, that her parents were the ones who could give me the most insight into Beth. My first thought was that I shouldn't intrude upon their grief at this time. Then it occurred to me I might be able to ease their pain a little if I told them how fond I'd become of Beth in the short time I knew her and that I harbored no bitterness toward her. After all, isn't one of the central beliefs of Christianity that of forgiveness? By now I'd realized it was pointless to be bitter, for the only one it would hurt would be me.

I decided to go the next day, Saturday, so I'd have a chance of catching both parents at home. And I wouldn't call them in advance even though I'd risk finding them gone. If I told them why I wanted to visit them, they'd probably turn me down. I'm sure they weren't in any frame of mind to talk to the victim of their daughter's scam. But I hoped I could alleviate their grief just a little bit.

I'd already planned it out when I remembered Cal and I had talked about getting together that day. He'd worry if he couldn't reach me, so I gave him a call.

"Well, hey," he said, "I was just about to call you. What should we do tomorrow? I was thinking about driving to Boca Raton."

"Can I have a rain check?"

"Feeling blue?" He could always detect the slightest nuance in my voice. "Doing something fun might cheer you up."

"I know you're going to think I've lost it, but I feel I have to go talk to Beth's parents. They live in Miami."

For a moment there was only silence. Then he said, "Do you know what you're getting into?"

"I've given it a lot of thought. I need to tell them I'd become very fond of Beth and, whatever her motive, I'm not bitter toward her. If you'd lost a daughter, wouldn't you want to hear that from the victim? Particularly under the circumstances?"

"But what about you? How is this going to affect you, Emma? Shouldn't you be trying to put this behind you?"

"That's exactly what I'm trying to do. Maybe by talking to them I can get some idea of who Beth really was. I just want to understand her. Then I can let it rest."

"Are you sure? Or is it going to stir the pot some more?" I sensed that Cal's patience and understanding were wearing thin. I was beginning to get a little annoyed by his oversolicitousness.

"Oh, Cal, give me the benefit of the doubt, will you? I need to do this."

"Okay. I didn't mean to come on like gangbusters. I'll let you off the hook if you'll agree to one thing."

"What's that?"

"You'll let me drive you to Miami."

"I don't know…"

"Think about it. Do you really want to face them by yourself?"

I thought about it. "I guess it could be pretty unnerving."

"I promise to keep my mouth shut if that's what you want. But I want to be there."

"Well…"

I could hear his television mumbling indistinctly in the background. Outside my window the gulls were screeching noisily as some child fed them bread crumbs on the beach. But Cal was silent, waiting for me to make up my mind.

"Okay," I said grudgingly because I felt this was something I should do alone. But if he wouldn't interfere when I got there, it would be nice to have his company on the way over and back.

"Good. Now, what time do you want to leave?"

"What is it, a four-hour drive?"

"About that."

"Let's leave about ten."

"Do you know where they live?"

"I'm going to call Detective Caronis and ask for their address. Tell him I want to send a sympathy card."

"A little deviousness, huh?"

"Didn't want to take a chance on his reaction."

"You're probably wise."

I called Caronis about ten.

"You're sending them a card?" He sounded surprised. "That's mighty gracious of you, considering."

"I'll just sign it a friend of Beth's. Have you found out anything new?"

"No. Just looks like a case of greed overcoming common sense. We'll keep an open file, but since nothing new has come to light it's on the back burner for now."

I was disappointed they weren't as curious about Beth's motives as I was. They readily accepted simple avarice as the answer.

By dinnertime I'd ironed the things I'd washed, run a few errands and packed a small bag. I was just sitting down to dinner when I heard a knock at the door.

When I opened it, there stood my son, Mark, looking tired and unutterably sad. He was holding a black soft-sided bag.

"Well, for goodness' sake," I exclaimed. "What are you doing here?" I had been seeing more of him since he moved to Tampa recently, but it wasn't like him to show up without calling first.

Every day he looked more and more like his father. The nose with the funny little point on the end. The ears that stuck out just a little too much. The endearing lopsided smile. That is when he was smiling, which he most certainly was not doing now.

He gave me a quick hug and a kiss, walked into the living room and sank onto the sofa, dropping his bag in the middle of the floor the way he used to drop his toys. "I had to get away. I didn't think you'd mind if I came. It's Cindy." Why did this not surprise me? She'd been the source of most of Mark's unhappiness.

I knew that he and Cindy had been attempting to reconcile. She'd fled Toledo a few months ago to get away from her lover, who'd been abusive. I took her in temporarily because she had nowhere else to go, although I had little use for her at the time. After all, she'd left Mark for the jerk who was now trying to hurt her. And Mark, not surprisingly, was most upset with me. But life takes strange twists and turns sometimes, and Cindy ended up saving my life. Perhaps Mark was swayed by gratitude when he suggested they give their marriage another chance.

"I was just sitting down to dinner. Have you eaten?"

"I'm not hungry."

"Well, come sit at the table with me while I eat."

He got up slowly like an old man and trailed behind me to the kitchen, sitting across from me at the tiny wrought-iron-and-glass table that seats two.

"I'm glad to see you," I said, not mentioning that the timing couldn't have been worse. "How long are you staying?"

He gave me a guilty look. "The whole week."

"How can you stay a whole week when you've only been working there a few months?"

He picked at a hangnail, refusing to look me in the eye. "I told them you were sick and needed me. They insisted I take the week off. They're the best employers I've ever had."

"But…" I started to ask how can you lie about it, when I realized I probably was going to have to do quite a bit of lying to him. "I hope they don't find out the truth," I finally said.

"They won't."

"I think the best tonic for you is to spend time on the beach and do a lot of resting up. You look tired."

"I am, Mom. I can't sleep."

He didn't want to talk about Cindy, now, that was obvious. Going through a second breakup must be excruciating, I thought. I finished eating, put the dishes in the dishwasher, and we went back to the living room to watch the news. It wasn't until it was over that he noticed my bag beside the front door.

"You going somewhere, Mom?" he asked.

I'd been pondering the idea of canceling the trip, but finally made the decision to go ahead with it. I needed to get my feelings under control before Mark and I had any long talks so I could decide what I dare say and what I should keep to myself. Even though my opinion about Cindy had changed dramatically since she had stayed with me, I still felt their relationship was doomed. When they were first married, I'd thought she was self-centered and totally out of touch with other people's feelings. But when I got to know her well, I realized her aloofness stemmed from low self-esteem. Cindy had trouble relating to others. I was enormously grateful for what she had done for me and became quite fond of her. But I knew in my heart that the two of them were unsuited to each other. Mark needed a lot of TLC which Cindy evidently couldn't provide, and Cindy required a lot of freedom which Mark was unwilling to cede to her.

So I told him, "I'm going to Miami in the morning. Just for overnight. I'll be back Sunday afternoon."

"I don't think a woman driving alone is safe anymore. Particularly not in this state."

"I'm going with Cal." Mark was fond of Cal, but I wasn't sure how he'd react to an overnight trip.

He looked at me for a moment in shocked silence. "An overnight trip?" he asked, disapproval apparent in his tone of voice.

"Come on, Mark. He's just helping me drive. There's nothing to it."

I could tell he thought otherwise, but he at least had

the sense not to say so. "What are you going to do in Miami?"

"We're visiting some people. I'm sure you can entertain yourself nicely till I get back."

Mark only grunted and said little for the rest of the evening. I guess he'd expected me to hold his hand for the next two days.

What worried me was that he'd find out about Beth and the money I'd lost. I'd have to clue in Cal somehow not to broach the subject in front of Mark. I was glad when Mark, claiming exhaustion, decided to go to bed early. Using the kitchen phone, I called Cal to tell him about my son's arrival.

"Do you want to cancel the trip?"

"No, I'm packed and ready to go. He'll just want to lie on the beach anyway. I wanted to warn you not to mention what we're doing. I've never told Mark about all this, and he's got enough problems without dumping mine on him."

"That's going to be tricky, isn't it?"

"Shouldn't be. Only you and the police know about my involvement."

"Okay. Hope you can pull it off. See you in the morning."

ELEVEN

I URGED MARK TO SLEEP IN, but he got up when I did. We had our orange juice, coffee and bagels out on the balcony. Since it was Saturday, a sizable crowd was already on the beach, and the smooth water winked and glittered in the bright sun.

At ten sharp, Cal knocked at the door. I invited him in and led him out to the balcony where Mark was finishing his coffee.

"Good to see you," Cal said, shaking his hand. "How are things in Tampa?"

Since Mark hadn't confirmed he and Cindy were splitting up, I hadn't mentioned it to Cal. But now I wished I had warned him not to ask that question.

"Okay, I guess," Mark said, his voice faltering. He couldn't look Cal in the eye.

I was standing behind Mark. Cal looked at me for some hint of what was going on, but I just shook my head. "He's always been partial to Crescent Beach," I said to break the tension. "Tampa can't compete with that."

"It's hard to beat," Cal agreed. "What do you say we get going, Emma?"

I gave Mark a hug. "Get rested up," I said. "I'll see you early tomorrow afternoon."

On the way out to the parking lot Cal asked, "What was going on in there? It seemed more like a funeral than a family visit."

"He hasn't said much, but I'm afraid his attempt at reconciliation with Cindy isn't working."

"There's a lot to be said for the girl, but I don't think they're meant for each other. They're too different."

"My thought exactly. I just hate that he has to go through the hurt a second time. You've been through a breakup. What's your advice? The main reason I decided to go ahead with this trip was because I don't know what to say to Mark. I'm afraid I'll only make it worse."

"Let him bring the subject up if he wants to. The important thing is to listen. There's not much anyone can say except they're sorry."

"Listen to what he has to say. Otherwise keep my mouth shut."

"That's about it."

"Thanks, Cal."

We'd agreed to take turns driving, and I drove the first leg to Naples. It was a pretty morning to be on the road even though, as with any interstate, I-75 is pretty boring. At least it keeps you out of the interminable strip shopping centers that line Route 41 much of the way south. Sometimes we chatted and sometimes we were quiet. We talked about our kids, politics and Michael Connelly mysteries, which we both adore.

Somehow we got to talking about volunteer work. Cal volunteers in the schools and at the library. I deliver Meals on Wheels but that's the extent of it. I used to volunteer at the hospital until Paul died. After that I couldn't bring myself to do it anymore. It was too depressing. I guess that's why I got so caught up in the search for truth about Beth. It seemed to give me a sense of purpose. I said as much to Cal.

"The one thing I'm sure of is that you believe in the basic goodness of people, Emma. The fact that you refuse to give up on Beth is proof of that. Anyone else would have written her off as a liar and thief, and cared not a whit about why she did it. But you're compelled to dog this thing in order to gain back your faith."

Well, I guess he had me there.

We stopped in Naples, the watering hole for many Fortune Five Hundred CEOs, for an early lunch. Everything about the city bespeaks money. The hotels and condominiums are grand, the landscaping lush and pristine, the beaches broad and not crowded. Nothing tacky dares raise its ugly head.

We found a charming little café and ordered salads.

Halfway through lunch Cal asked, "Have you decided what you're going to say to Beth's parents?"

"Uh...no. I wanted to meet them before I decide how to approach it. If they're as open and warm as she was, it shouldn't be too hard."

"And if they aren't?"

I thought for a minute. Then I smiled what I hoped was a goofy smile. "Guess I'll just have to charm them."

The minute it was out of my mouth, I realized how taste-less that sounded. After all, they'd just lost their daugh-ter.

Cal tactfully said nothing.

He took over the wheel as we headed across the state on the interstate bordered by miles and miles of flat wet-lands that stretch as far as the eye could see. Somehow I'd always envisioned the Everglades as very tropical, but the only tropical-looking places were the hummocks, rounded knolls that rose up only a few feet but supported dense growth. The drive seemed interminable before we came to the western edge of the Miami urban area, but that was probably due to the numbing sameness of the scenery.

Apprehension was building inside me the closer we got to the Wilkinsons'. What seemed like a good idea the day before now loomed like a disaster in waiting. How would they react to me? They'd probably want to throw me out of the house. What was I going to say that would put the best face on my visit? I'd jumped into this pretty mindlessly when it came right down to it. I won-dered whatever possessed me. If Cal hadn't been along, I would have turned around and driven home. But I was too embarrassed to admit I'd clearly not thought this through.

Reluctantly I read the city map I'd bought and di-rected Cal toward Kendall, a suburb on the southeast side of Miami. Due to heavy traffic it took nearly as long to cross Miami as it did to drive across the state.

We eventually found the street, 124th, and the Wil-

kinsons' address. It was an upper-middle-class neigh-
borhood with relatively new stucco homes with tile roofs
and small lots. There were two cars, a Toyota and a
Subaru, parked in the driveway, which I took as a sign
that both Beth's parents were home. Cal parked at the
curb and followed me up to the dark green front door.
By this time I was almost sick with apprehension.

A woman in her fifties answered my knock. She was
wearing a checked blouse with a denim skirt, leather
sandals, and her hair was the same auburn as Beth's
without a single gray strand. Her resemblance to her
daughter was striking, the same beautiful complexion
and huge brown eyes.

"Mrs. Wilkinson?" I asked, although there was no
doubt in my mind that it was Beth's mother.

"Yes?" She appeared nervous. I wondered if she
thought we were reporters here to gather information
for a sensational story about her daughter.

"I knew Beth," I said gently. Tears welled up in Mrs.
Wilkinson's eyes, and her lower lip began to tremble. "I
wanted to give you my condolences in person," I continued. "May we come in?"

She hesitated a moment, a look of fear in her eyes.
Then apparently her ingrained sense of good manners
won out. She stepped back and motioned us into the
foyer, then led us toward the back of the house where
a kitchen–family room looked out upon a caged pool.
A man was sitting on a couch watching a golf game
on TV. He shut it off with a remote and stood to greet
us. He was fairly tall, slender, almost anemic-looking,

and had only a fringe of hair that was completely gray, though he appeared no older than his wife. His features were sharp, as though chiseled from some exceedingly resistant material; his small eyes were penetrating and gave me the uneasy feeling he was looking directly into my soul. He wore gray slacks and a long-sleeved dress shirt buttoned up to the neck even on this warm day.

"This is my husband, Bruce," she said, "and I'm Patty."

"I'm Emma Daniels from Sarasota."

Cal stepped forward to shake Bruce's hand. "And I'm Cal Murray, also from Sarasota."

"Won't you sit down? Can I get you something to drink?" Patty was beginning to flutter nervously now, picking up newspapers off the floor, straightening pillows, carrying an empty glass to the sink. The all-white kitchen was sleek and modern and was separated from the rest of the room by a long counter. The family room was furnished in Victorian pieces, which seemed very much at odds with the architectural style of the house that featured vaulted ceilings and open spaces.

We both declined her offer of a drink and sat on matching carved walnut side chairs with needlepoint seats that faced the wine-colored velvet couch. The carved back of the chair dug into my back and caused me to sit up straight. I noticed that Cal looked pretty rigid, too. This was not a room to relax in.

Patty was still picking up discarded magazines and dirty ashtrays when Bruce said, "Come sit down, Patty." His tone left no doubt who was in charge in this family.

She abruptly laid down the ashtray and magazine she was holding and sat beside him.

He then turned to me. "Now what is it we can do for you?" There was a veneer of hospitality to his tone, but underneath I detected an unspoken ultimatum: whatever it is it had better be good. I don't like to have my time wasted.

"I wanted to tell you how deeply sorry I am about Beth's death. I only knew her a short while, but I felt close to her. I thought she was a special person."

Patty began to weep silently into a handkerchief she'd pulled from her pocket.

"I see. And how did you know Beth?" Bruce asked, bringing me to the point of my visit much sooner than I'd wanted.

I saw Cal glance surreptitiously my way as if asking, "Okay, now what are you going to do?"

"I, ah...I..." I couldn't think how to put it so it wouldn't upset Patty and enrage Bruce. Already I could envision each of their reactions.

"Are you with Ringling?" Patty asked as she wiped her eyes, sensing my uneasiness.

"Well, uh, no. I met Beth on the beach. She was painting a wonderful picture of Crescent Beach where I live." Maybe I could work up to this slowly.

"Are you a painter, too?" Patty wanted to know.

"Don't I wish. No, I was just admiring her work." I stopped, again not knowing how to continue.

We all sat in silence for a moment. Then Bruce spoke up. "So you drove all the way from Sarasota to tell us that? That you met her on the beach and liked her painting?" His voice was charged with skepticism.

"Not exactly." I could feel the sweat run down my sides in spite of the air-conditioning. "Actually, what I wanted to tell you was that I was the one she got the money from."

Patty's eyes were wide in horror now, and Bruce's face had gone from almost ashen to red with rage.

Before I had a chance to say anything further, Bruce stood up, his hands balled into fists at his sides, his sharp features made sharper still by his wrath. His little eyes were bulging. "So you came here expecting us to pay you off, did you? My daughter was an adult. I am not responsible for her debts or her transgressions. You've got a lot of nerve coming here to extort money from us when we're in mourning. What kind of a person are you anyway?"

I was speechless. I never dreamed he'd think such a thing.

Patty was sobbing uncontrollably into her handkerchief.

For the first time, Cal entered the conversation. "Mr. Wilkinson, sit down, will you, and let's discuss this calmly." Bruce glared at him and returned to his seat slowly. Cal continued. "Emma intended no such thing. What she wanted you to know was that she has forgiven Beth. In the time they spent together, she became very fond of your daughter and was devastated by her death. She feels there had to be some compelling reason for

Beth to take her money because it seemed so totally out of character."

"Oh, it was, it was," Patty said, wiping her eyes. "My little girl wasn't like that."

Bruce looked at Patty crossly. "That's the trouble, Patty. She wasn't our little girl anymore. She got in with those heathens at the art school, and they ruined her. God knows what kind of things she was doing over there."

"What do you mean they ruined her?" I asked. I'd finally regained my composure.

"I know how they carry on at those places, painting filthy art. I'd heard they even let students pose nude. They wallow in pornography. The devil must be running rampant in that place."

Oh, God, I thought, I hope he never finds out Beth was one of the models.

"She was always such an obedient child," Patty spoke up. "She went to Sunday School and church and read the Bible and always honored her mother and father like the Bible says. But when it came time to go to college, she changed. She wouldn't listen to us when we tried to get her to go to a good Christian school."

"She defied our wishes and went to Ringling instead," her husband interrupted. "That was the beginning of the end as far as I'm concerned. It was all downhill after that."

"I talked to one of her teachers," I said. "He thought..."

"You even went over to talk to a teacher?" Patty asked incredulously.

"Yes. I wanted to find out more about her. You don't understand, but I'm haunted about what happened. I'm trying to figure it all out."

Bruce looked at me as though I were some strange species he'd never seen before. "You barely knew her, and you'd go to all this trouble?"

"Yes, that's why I'm here. Not to add to your sorrow, but to try to understand your daughter because she made such an impression on me. Anyway, I talked to her teacher and he, too, thought she was very special. He said she was popular with both faculty and students. Also that she had a very strong desire to finish her education there. Do you think she might have been trying to get money for tuition?"

"She was very strong willed," Bruce said, his brow furrowed, "especially since we started arguing over college. If she wanted something bad enough, she usually could find a way to get it. She probably picked up all kinds of evil ways over there in Sarasota."

Patty seemed more nervous now than ever. She was twisting her handkerchief to the point I thought she'd rip it in two. She looked at her husband fearfully and then turned to me. "No, I don't think that was it. I'd told her recently I thought I could get enough money together for her to return to school."

"You what?" Bruce roared. "You'd give her money behind my back? And to go to that godforsaken place?"

Her face colored and she looked down at her lap. Finally she looked him in the eye. "She wanted it so badly. I couldn't stand to see her so unhappy. And I couldn't see how it was all that bad. I told her I was going to ask my uncle Brady for some money. He's got plenty, and he's always said he'd help out if I ever needed anything."

"My God, Patty. I can't believe you'd aid and abet Beth when you knew how much I was against her going there. No wonder the girl went astray."

Patty was crying again. I wanted so much to hug her. Her husband was a real case. I decided it was time we left before the situation got out of control.

I started to rise. "I didn't mean to cause any problems. I'd thought it might help if you knew how I felt about your daughter, and that I've forgiven her. That is what Jesus taught, isn't it? Forgiveness?" I directed this mainly at Bruce.

He stood up, frowning, apparently too angry to reply.

Patty wiped her eyes again and stood and shook my hand. "Thanks, Emma," she said. "That means a lot to me." She shook Cal's hand, too. "And thank you, Cal."

She walked us to the door. Bruce didn't move or say goodbye.

I gave her the hug before I left. "Hang in there," I said, aware how trite that sounded. But what else could I tell her? She lived with a son of a bitch and just lost her daughter under very questionable circumstances. There was not much else she could do but hang in there.

As we crossed the yard, a Geo Tracker pulled into the drive behind the Toyota and a teenage boy got out. He, too, had his mother's auburn hair, but his features were more like his dad's. He looked at us curiously as he got out of his car.

"Are you Beth's brother?" I asked.

"Yes, I'm Raeford, better known as Ray."

I glanced at Cal, but his features were noncommittal. He wouldn't give me a clue as to how he thought I should proceed.

"Ray, I'm Emma Daniels and this is Cal Murray. We're from Sarasota. I'd love to talk to you about your sister. But your parents are so grief-stricken that I'd rather not do it here. Could we by any chance meet you somewhere else?"

He glanced at his watch. It was now almost four. "I could meet you at the McDonald's on Bird Avenue around eight."

"That would be great. We'll see you there."

When we got in the car, Cal said, "I apologize."

"Whatever for?"

"I said I'd keep my mouth shut in there."

"I'm awfully glad you didn't. Bruce really shook me up. I didn't know what to say."

"What a jerk."

"But she was nice."

"Too much under his thumb. I'm surprised she had gumption enough to go to Uncle Brady for money."

"Me, too. But our trip has been worthwhile."

"Even with Bruce's little tantrum?"

"Yes. Now I know Beth didn't do it to get money for school. So I've got to find out what she did need the money for."

Cal looked at me with a wry smile. "I thought this visit was supposed to be the end of it."

"Well—" I smiled back "—I guess I lied."

TWELVE

WE FOUND A DAYS INN NOT too far away and got two non-smoking rooms. I asked for an upstairs room because I hate hearing people walk around over my head. Cal's was next door.

"It's just four-thirty," Cal said. "Do you want to drive around and see the beaches? Then we can eat and meet Ray at the McDonald's by eight."

Cal was familiar with the tourist areas of Miami, having written articles about them. He took me to see the restored Art Deco buildings of South Beach. I was amazed. I'd remembered how the area catered mostly to old folks years ago, but we hardly saw a wrinkled brow. Instead we were surrounded by multitudes of beautiful and athletic young people showing off their perfect bodies in skimpy dress. He said it is quite the mecca now for photographic modeling, with the exceptional light and the unique pastel buildings. In-line skaters moved through the crowds with ease and grace, and Cal told me people partied around the clock. It was enough to make me feel like a centenarian. The place has been revived with a vengeance.

We found a small restaurant near Kendall that advertised stone crab claws, a succulent treat I can't resist.

The marvelous dinner almost made up for the bad experience with Bruce Wilkinson.

We got to the McDonald's a little before eight o'clock and Ray had not yet arrived. We each ordered a cup of coffee and sat by a window watching for the Geo Tracker. Ray was about fifteen minutes late.

"Sorry," he said, sitting down beside Cal. "I was having an argument with my dad."

"Because you were seeing us?" I asked.

"Nah. He doesn't know about that. We argue all the time about everything. I'm getting out of here as soon as I'm eighteen. I don't know how Beth managed to stick around until she was almost twenty."

"Can we buy you something to eat?" Cal asked.

"Thanks, no. Just got up from a big supper at home."

"About Beth," I said. "What did she do after she graduated from high school?"

"She was a waitress. Saved enough for her first-year tuition and then went to Ringling. Of course at the time Mom and Dad didn't know she'd made up her mind to go there. That's why she stayed at home, so she wouldn't have to spend her money for rent and food and stuff. Though she did have to pay Mom something for room and board. To tell you the truth, I think Mom secretly gave it back to her when she left." He gave us a sad smile. "So how do you know her?"

"I guess your parents didn't tell you. I'm the one she took the money from."

"No joke?" Ray seemed genuinely surprised.

"No joke," I said.

He shook his head, incredulity in his eyes. "I still can't believe she'd do a thing like that. I know Dad thinks she got all screwed up over there, but I know better. I visited her last year. She loved school so much she was willing to work alternate years to get enough money together to pay her way. She always said you appreciate things more when you have to work for them."

"Ray, I need to ask you. Your sister was so believable, so convincing. Had she always played fast and loose with the truth? I mean she seems to have charmed everyone in Sarasota, and they all are certain she was Little Miss Goody Two-Shoes. She sure had me persuaded."

Ray took off the visor cap he had on backward and thoughtfully fingered the bill of it as he talked. "Beth loved to act. She had the lead in most of the school plays. Hell, she was so good she probably could have made it a career, except painting always came first. But I never saw her use her acting skills to con anybody." He shook his head. "She probably would have got into a lot less trouble with Mom and Dad if she'd conned them once in a while. But she always told it like it was." He hesitated a minute as though a new thought had occurred to him. "Of course, when she was living at home, she didn't tell them she planned to go to Ringling. But she didn't lie about it, either. She just didn't discuss it. And that's what I don't understand. How could she make up all that stuff? I know what you must think of her, but that wasn't what she was like at all."

I wondered. Perhaps her whole life had been nothing but artifice and even her brother had bought into it.

"Did you know your mother was going to ask your uncle Brady for tuition money so Beth could go back to Ringling?" I wondered what his reaction would be to that.

"God, no! Does my dad know?"

"She told him this afternoon."

"Oh, Christ, no wonder he was in such a foul mood. I guess Mom is more of a softy than Beth or I realized. But usually she feels like she has to go along with Dad on everything."

I decided it was time to ask the Big Question. Not that I expected much in the way of an answer. "Ray, do you have any idea at all why Beth would come up with such an elaborate scheme to get money?"

Ray closed his eyes, sadness making him look less like his dad and more like his mother. "I've been trying to figure that out since we heard about it. Sis and I were very close. She was the best. I can't explain it at all."

"Is there anyone you know of who was close to her in recent weeks?"

"Let me think." He picked up a paper napkin lying on the table and started folding it into smaller and smaller squares, as if trying to wrest from the flimsy paper some kind of knowledge or truth. "She'd been seeing some guy—can't think of his name—at school. Don't know if she was still seeing him or not."

"Try to remember his name. It might be someone

I could talk to." Though, I had suspicions it could be Emile Szostak and I figured he'd already said everything he was going to say to me.

Ray closed his eyes and concentrated. "Olds…Olden something." He made a fist and knocked on his forehead. "Damn, why can't I think of it? Wait a minute. I think it's Oldenburg." He opened his eyes and grinned. "That's right. Timothy Oldenburg."

"I talked to one of her teachers who seemed to know her pretty well. He never mentioned a boyfriend."

"I think she kept it kind of quiet. Wanted to make sure word didn't get back to the parents. They probably wouldn't have approved of him since he was an artist, too. God, they probably wouldn't approve of anyone."

"Know anything about him? Where he lived?"

"Um, no. In fact, she was kind of mysterious about him even to me. I took it to mean she liked him a lot. She always kept her mouth shut about the ones she liked. Guess she thought I'd tease her."

"Anybody else you know of?"

"That's the only name I can come up with. She didn't pal around a lot. She didn't have time."

"Well, Ray, thanks for talking to me. I'm really sorry about what happened to Beth. I thought I was helping her out, but it seems that my giving her money did just the opposite."

"You couldn't have known." His voice started to tremble. I thought we should leave before he broke down. I knew he wouldn't want us to see that.

I rose from my seat and Cal followed suit. "We've

got to go now," I said and put my hand on Ray's shoulder. "Thanks again."

He got up to let Cal out, and Cal shook his hand before we left. "Good luck, Ray," he said.

Ray was still looking forlornly out the window when we pulled out of the parking lot.

"He seems like a nice kid," Cal said as we drove toward the motel.

"Yes, he does. He's got it tough, too. I don't think his dad has ever been easy to get along with. And I'm sure he's a real martinet now."

It was only nine o'clock when we got to the motel. "Want to see if they have any good movies on TV? We could watch it in my room," I said, wanting to be gracious after he drove me across the state.

"Why don't I go down to the corner to the convenience store and get some popcorn or something?"

He was back in a few minutes with a huge bag of cheese popcorn and a six-pack of cold beer.

"Is beer okay or do you want a coke?" he asked.

"Beer would be fine."

I filled my ice bucket to keep the unopened beer cold, and Cal brought his to use as a popcorn bowl. We propped up the pillows on the separate beds and settled in to watch *Magnificent Obsession* with Rock Hudson and Jane Wyman on AMC.

As the evening wore on I had two cans of beer. That's one more than I usually have, but sadness was creeping insidiously through my system like a virus. Before I realized it, I was crying and feeling really foolish about it.

"What's wrong?" Cal had suddenly noticed my tears.

I waved toward the movie screen to indicate the movie was the source of my sorrow. My throat was too tight to say much.

"Too bad there wasn't a comedy on," he said.

If only that would have made a difference. But I was sure it would not. All the sorrow of the past year compounded by the experience of the past two weeks had accumulated into one miserable lump of unhappiness in my chest, making it hard to breathe. Without even thinking, I got off my bed and lay down beside Cal, throwing my arm around his body and hugging him to me, hoping his warmth might dissolve the wretchedness inside me.

For a few seconds he failed to respond, then his arm encircled me and he whispered in my ear, "Emma, don't cry. I'm here for you."

But that unleashed a veritable flood of tears that had been dammed up too long. Cal held me tightly, crooning, "Okay, then. Let it all out, let it all out." Finally I lay back on the pillow in exhaustion.

Cal propped himself up on one elbow. "I need to tell you something, Emma." His voice was grave.

I swiped at my eyes to clear them. "Tell me what?"

"You probably think I either have incredible self-control or else I don't find you all that desirable."

Whoa. This was getting into dangerous waters. I was becoming more and more attracted to Cal.

He looked uncomfortable now; he seemed to be having trouble knowing what to say. "Neither is true,

Emma. You mean so much to me I haven't known how to tell you this."

"My God, Cal. What is it?"

"I've had prostate cancer."

I threw my arms around him. "Oh, no. Are you okay?" I realized I couldn't bear the thought of losing him.

He pulled back. "I've been given a clean bill of health. But I'm not totally okay, if you get my drift." His eyes held incredible sadness. "I was sure that once I told you, I'd lose you."

I pulled him into my arms once again and hugged him tightly. "No way. You can't get off the hook that easily."

"Now it's my turn to cry," he said and brushed a tear away.

"Why don't you spend the night," I said. "I'm not adverse to snuggling."

Cal finally smiled. "Snuggle it shall be."

THIRTEEN

IT WAS TWO O'CLOCK BEFORE we got back to Sarasota after treating ourselves to a generous Sunday brunch in Kendall. It was a pleasant trip, though we didn't talk much. We didn't need to. The ogre had been pulled out of the closet and exposed, and we had dealt with it. I can't say that I wasn't taken by surprise, because I was. On the other hand, Paul had been my one and only lover, and I'd always felt that I would somehow betray his memory if I made love with someone else. Silly and old-fashioned, I guess, but the way I felt nonetheless. So that went a long way toward alleviating my disappointment. Cal was a wonderful man in so many ways, and I felt so lucky to have him in my life. Many women don't have anyone they can even snuggle with.

When we got to La Hacienda, I didn't ask Cal to come up to the condo. He got my bag out, gave me a bear hug and said he'd give me a call.

When I walked in the door, Mark was lying on the couch asleep. He was wearing a polo shirt and shorts and was barefoot. The Sunday paper was scattered around him on the floor, and the coffee table had an empty coffee cup and a plate with toast crumbs and egg remnants. I walked into the kitchen and there were dirty dishes from the night before in the sink. Evidently he'd forgotten how to use a dishwasher. Considering it was one of his jobs when he was a kid, I was surprised. It didn't look to me as though he'd left the condo while I'd been gone.

I went in my bedroom to change into shorts, and by the time I came out Mark was awake. He was stacking the paper into a neat pile.

"How was your trip?" he asked, rubbing his chin, which hadn't been shaved since he arrived.

"Fine."

"How were your friends?"

"Well, they weren't my friends. Just some people I needed to talk to." Oh, damn, why did I say that? I knew better. Anything with a hint of mystery would just pique his interest.

"What did you need to talk to them about?"

I knew it! I led myself right into the trap.

"It has to do with business matters, Mark." Pretty far-fetched, but my stolen thirty-six thousand was monkey business if nothing else.

He looked hurt. Again. "You've always come to me for advice before. Can't you do that now?" I'm sure he wouldn't have said that except he was feeling rejected by Cindy and now must have felt his mother was rejecting him, too.

"Hon, it's nothing you can help me with. Don't worry about it."

He looked at me sadly and said nothing.

"Look, why don't we take a walk on the beach. Have you been out on the beach at all?"

"Nah. Just hung out around the house."

"Well, come on, then. That's what you do in Sarasota. You can lie around the house at home." And then I felt like biting my tongue once more, since reminding him of home also reminded him of his troubles. This was going to be very tricky, trying to avoid mentioning anything to do with Cindy or my experience with Beth.

He put on some sandals, and we took the elevator down to the lobby. Once on the beach, we headed south. It was a lovely, vibrant day, the kind of day Florida beaches were made for—warm enough to swim, yet with a delightful breeze that caressed our faces as we strolled along the water's edge.

We were within sight of Point of Rocks when we encountered Jean and Ross Jacobs walking north.

"Emma, hello. And, Mark, it's good to see you again," Jean greeted us in her effusive manner. "And where is your wife, Mark? Is she one of those who are afraid of getting sunburned?"

Oh, Lord. I'd told Jean that they'd gotten back together. Now I wish I hadn't.

I could see Mark's face redden. "Uh, no. She's back in Tampa. Had to work."

He managed that very gracefully, I thought.

"Oh, I'm so sorry. We'll have to get together sometime." Jean was the quintessential gracious neighbor and hostess.

"I'd like that," Mark answered, but I could see the

tenseness in his jaw. I knew he didn't want to have to pretend for anyone that his life was okay.

The Jacobses went on, and Mark and I explored the jutting layers of stone at Point of Rocks. I found several nice olive shells and a couple of whelks. But by and large the shelling had always been better at Turtle Beach at the south end of Siesta Key. It seems to catch most of the sea detritus as the waves roll up over its spit of sand. Mark surprised me with a small starfish. I hadn't seen any on the beach since the night soon after Paul and I moved here, when a powerful storm littered the beach with hundreds of starfish of all sizes. It looked as though the stars had fallen out of heaven that night.

We were sitting on the sand admiring our finds when a woman approached us. She was wearing a bikini that left little to the imagination and did even less to enhance her plump body. Her hair was bleached almost white with black roots making a stripe in her part down the center of her skull.

"Excuse me," she said. "I'm just visiting here. Is this the place where they found that girl's body?"

Mark looked at her with a shocked expression. Why are people so infinitely curious about gruesome events?

"No," I said, "it was up at the north end of the island."

"Do you know if they ever found out if she planned that whole scam herself or if other people were in it, too?"

"I have no idea." I wanted her to go away, but I didn't want to be too uncivil in front of Mark. I turned to him. "Think it's time to walk back to the condo?" I began to get up before he answered. I busied myself gathering my shells with my back to the woman. But she didn't get it.

"I heard she got a bunch of money offa somebody but they never found it."

This time I gave her the evil eye. "I really know nothing about it." I grabbed Mark's arm—he was standing now and looking bewildered by my actions—and started walking.

When we were out of hearing range, he said to me, "Why were you so rude to that woman?"

"Oh, I don't know. I hate people coming up to you and asking dumb questions. Besides, she was obnoxious." Actually, I was ashamed of myself for treating her so badly.

Mark looked at me curiously but said nothing. My desire to keep him in the dark was causing me to behave in uncharacteristic ways. I knew I must think through what I was going to say or do rather than react blindly to every situation.

We didn't speak the rest of the way home. It wasn't until dinner that he brought it up again. I'd cooked Hungarian goulash, one of his favorite dishes, and was looking forward to a pleasant meal, when he said, "What's the story on the dead girl they found on the key?"

My heart sank. I was hoping he'd forgotten about it. "Some girl drowned. Apparently she'd gone out in a small boat when the small-craft warnings were up, and it overturned."

"Well, what did that woman mean about a scam?"

"Oh, Lord, Mark, I don't know. There's enough bad news out there without reading about something like that."

He looked at me with concern. "You don't have to get all bent out of shape just because I asked."

I hadn't realized how cross I'd sounded. The more I tried to avoid the subject, the more I drew him in because of my petulance. "I'm sorry, hon. It's coming up on the anniversary of your dad's death, and I'm kind of cranky. But I'm working on my attitude. Honestly."

He smiled and patted my hand. "I know, Mom. I shouldn't criticize you. I'm not exactly a laugh a minute myself these days."

Mentally I gave a sigh of relief. I apparently wiggled out of that one safely. We watched TV for a while that evening, eliminating the need for much conversation, but I was sure it was going to be tricky to get through the week without stirring things up again.

Around nine-thirty, Mark said he'd like to walk on the beach again. "I think it will help me get to sleep. Want to go along?"

"Thanks, hon, but I'm tired. You go ahead."

After he'd left, I pulled the phone number I'd found on Casey Key from my wallet and studied it again, wondering if it could be Timothy Oldenburg's. It seemed like a good possibility, and that would simplify contacting him.

I dialed it and a man answered on the third ring.

"Is Timothy there?" I asked.

The next thing I knew, I had a dial tone. It might have been an accident, but I didn't think so. How strange.

I called Cal. "You know that phone number I found on Casey Key?"

"Yeah," he said.

"I thought it might belong to Beth's boyfriend, Timothy. So I just now called it."

"And...?"

"A man answered, and when I asked for Timothy, he hung up. Don't you think that's weird? Or do you think he was just rude?"

"I don't particularly like the sound of that."

"Well, I'm not worried about it. After all, I didn't give my name. I just wondered what was going on."

"But, Emma. He probably has caller ID and knows it was you who called."

"Oh, God. That never occurred to me. I can't keep up with all this technology. I still think answering machines are on the cutting edge."

"You've got to be careful, Emma. You don't know what you're dealing with."

This kind of talk was making me crazy. I hadn't been the least anxious about my well-being up to this point. But Cal's voice was as solemn as I'd ever heard. "Let's not get too hyper and let our imaginations run away with us," I told him. "The police don't seem concerned about me."

"I know, Emma. But that doesn't necessarily mean they shouldn't. I just think you need to be cautious. Please."

I was touched by his concern. "Sure, you know I will."

It wasn't until I'd gone to bed that Cal's admonition to be careful really sank in. Alone and in the dark, my hard-won self-confidence began to dissolve into a state of insecurity. It was much the same as the night that Paul died, when I lay alone in our king-size bed wondering how I could possibly go on without him. It was like being suspended in a state of precariousness from which I could never escape. Every simple daily act was fraught with uncertainty and fear. But, over the year, I'd been winning the battle to regain my self-assurance, and I was damned if I was going to let a stupid phone call wipe it all away.

I WOKE EARLY BUT MARK slept in. The morning light dissolved most of my feelings of vulnerability, if not every last one. I was determined not to knuckle under to my fear.

I went out on the beach for a while. I was worried that it would stir too many memories, but the surf and the shorebirds and the view all filled me with a sense of repose. It was a very healing experience to be there, something I'd learned after Paul's death.

I returned home to find that Mark was still asleep. That was good; maybe he'd learned to relax a little. I had breakfast, read the paper and then decided I needed to do a couple of things before Mark woke up.

First, I looked in the phone directory for Timothy Oldenburg, but he was not listed. That wasn't too surprising. He was probably in a dorm or boardinghouse.

Next, I decided to call the Ringling School of Art. I

asked for the Admissions Department, and a pleasant voice came on the line.

"I'm calling to inquire about a student. Do you have someone enrolled by the name of Timothy Oldenburg?"

"Sorry, but we can't give out that information."

Well, damn. I guess it was the Privacy Act. Now what could I do? Maybe Szostak would know something, and he'd given me his number. I called it but all I got was voice mail asking me to leave a message. I left a brief one simply asking him to return my call.

I was sitting in the living room trying to decide what to do next, when someone rang my doorbell.

I was sorry that I opened it. Mark's wife, Cindy, was standing there. Dressed in a frumpy sundress, with sunglasses perched atop hair that didn't look like it had seen a comb in a couple of days, she gave me a weak smile.

"Hi, Emma."

"Hi, Cindy." I didn't want to invite her in, but what could I do? I stood back and gestured her into the room. I had very mixed emotions about this. We'd established a pretty good relationship between us in recent months, but she still was putting Mark through hell. Talk about being between a rock and a hard place.

"Is Mark here?"

"He is, Cindy. But I'm not sure he wants to see you."

She walked over and plopped herself down on the sofa. I was afraid Mark would hear us, and then who knew what would happen.

"Well, I need to see him."

"May I ask why?"

"Honestly, Emma, I don't think it's any of your business." Her voice had an edge to it.

I almost physically recoiled at that. I thought we were pretty good friends, but apparently not as good as I thought.

"I'm sorry, I didn't mean to intrude."

"Intrude into what?" I turned around and Mark was standing at the edge of the bedroom hallway. He was wearing a pair of bathing trunks and apparently had been headed for the beach. "What the hell are you doing here, Cindy?"

"I need some money, Mark. I'm flat broke."

"Then you shouldn't quit your job every couple of months or so. You must have one lousy résumé, the way you constantly leave jobs without giving them notice."

"You're my husband, Mark. You're supposed to support me."

"You should have thought of that when you went back to jumping into other guys' beds. You made a promise to me when we got back together. It lasted how long? Three lousy months or so?"

Cindy's face started to cloud up. She could turn on the tears without too much trouble when she wanted to. "I'm sorry, Mark, honestly. I try. I really try."

"Suck it up!" Mark declared angrily. "I'm going to the beach." And he stomped out the door. The next thing I knew, Cindy ran after him. I hoped they wouldn't argue on their way out to the beach. I didn't need the whole building to know their business.

Well, so much for a calm and peaceful morning. I

was glad Mark left, because I didn't want to be in the middle of their argument. It was too draining. I hated getting drawn into other people's fights.

FOURTEEN

MARK CAME BACK ABOUT two hours later. It was lunch-time and I'd prepared a seafood salad for us, enough for three if I needed it, but he was alone. He went directly into the bedroom without saying a word and came out a short while later wearing shorts and a tee. I'd already dished up the food for us.

After we sat eating for a few minutes, I asked, "Want to talk about it?"

He didn't say anything at first. Finally he heaved a sigh and said, "She promised me she would get psychiatric help. I told her I wouldn't get back together with her until she'd proven she would do it and stick with it for a while."

"And you're paying for it, of course."

He shook his head. "Yes, if it will help her. I owe her that."

"You think so?"

"Mom, she had one screwed-up childhood. It's no wonder she's so messed up. I think we could make a go of it if she can get herself straightened out."

I had an awful lot of doubts about that, but maybe Paul and I raised him right if he was trying so very hard to make a go of his marriage. But I wondered how many times he could keep on forgiving her.

"Well, it's your call, of course, Mark. I think it's beyond noble of you to stick by her time after time."

His face reddened. "Don't make a martyr of me, Ma. I can't be easy to live with. I have plenty of faults, too."

Of course, being his mother, I didn't believe that. I thought he was pretty close to perfect. But that's what moms do.

Even though he and Cindy had come to a truce of sorts, he decided to spend the rest of the week with me. "I can't go back and tell them you've miraculously recovered," he said. "So I'm going to play a little more hooky. Besides, since Cindy left me last month, I've been working horrendous hours, and I do need a break. I told her to find a residential unit where she could work out not only her emotional problems, but deal with her addiction to prescription drugs, as well. We'll never be able to put our marriage back together until she can stay with the treatment to the end."

I wasn't going to argue with that.

Mark left to run some errands after lunch, and I went out on the balcony to try and pull myself back together—once again. After going through such an emotional roller coaster with Beth, I sure hadn't needed this scene with Cindy. All I could pray for was that she would do as she promised and get the help she needed.

Emile Szostak called me at the end of his lunch break.

"Mrs. Daniels? Do you have some kind of news?"

"Not really. However, I did talk to Beth's brother,

who said he thought Beth might have been going out with a Timothy Oldenburg, but I haven't been able to track him down. Do you know him? Do you have any idea where he lives?"

"He was in one of my classes last year. If you'll wait a minute, I keep a roster of all my students and their addresses." I guess he wasn't bothered that he was violating privacy issues. I think he'd been too upset by Beth's death to worry about that.

"That would be great."

He gave me a number on Patterson Street, which he informed me was just north of the school. "I think I heard that he dropped out of school last semester, but I'm not sure."

"Well, maybe he's working in town. At least I will check it out."

"Keep in touch, will you?"

"Absolutely," I said. "And thanks for your help."

After putting on flowered Bermuda shorts with a white tee, I left Mark a note saying I'd gone to get groceries. I drove up the Trail to Patterson, which was easy to find since Emile had told me that Mel's Drive-Thru was on the corner. A huge replica of an ice-cream cone, one could hardly miss it. Its location near the art school seemed quite appropriate; it was a gem of '50s kitsch. I turned and headed east till I found the number. A 1920s bungalow, its front porch enclosed with jalousie windows, it was fairly down-at-the-heels: peeling paint, sagging front steps. The grass was losing out to the weeds in the tiny yard, and the few shrubs around the foundation were unkempt. I parked my car around the corner and climbed the uneven steps to knock on the front door. It had once been white but was now gray from years' accumulation of grime. I knocked twice before the door opened slightly, and a grossly obese woman peered at me through the crack. She wore her brown hair skimmed back from her face into a ludicrous topknot, and her double chins hung down from her face over the neckline of her tentlike dress that barely contained the mound of flesh that was her body. She was breathing heavily from the effort of walking.

"Yes?" she asked pleasantly.

"My name is Emma Daniels. I'm trying to find Timothy Oldenburg and was given this address."

She opened the door wide. "Why, come on in, honey." Huffing and puffing, she led me across the porch that served as a greenhouse crammed with dozens of pots of bromeliads and pothos and African violets toward a tiny parlor on the right front of the house. Although a little shabby and timeworn, it was surprisingly charming in its cluttered ambience. There was one large overstuffed chair, draped with an old paisley shawl, into which she gingerly lowered her bulk. The rest of the chairs, mismatched antique side chairs in cherry and walnut, clearly would not hold her weight. The dark-stained mantel held a collection of old pitchers, at least one of which was Wedgewood, the windows were draped with what appeared to be lace tablecloths, and ruffled pillows and crocheted doilies and an assortment of old knickknacks were arranged everywhere with an artistic eye.

It was evident she cared about her home but had neither the money nor the physical ability to keep up the exterior.

She gestured for me to sit in a chair across from her as she struggled to get her breath from her exertion.

Finally she said, "I'm Regina Delvecchio. I run a little boardinghouse here to keep body and soul together." She giggled. "As you can see, I have quite a bit of body to keep together."

I just smiled back. What could I say?

"So you're looking for Timmy?"

I'd concocted a story to tell her to avoid having to go into the long, sad true one. "My family and his were neighbors years ago. I'd heard he was at Ringling, and since I moved here recently, I thought I'd look him up."

"Oh, that's sweet," she said, looking delighted. "Timmy's such a dear boy."

"Would he be here now?"

Her smile vanished. "Well, no. To tell the truth, he don't live here anymore. He took it so hard when Beth drowned, he went into kind of a funk. Did you hear about that poor girl they found out on Siesta Key?"

"I remember hearing something about that."

"Oh, it was terrible. They was lovers, you see. She sometimes come over here with Timmy. She was always so nice to me, not like them other young people who act like I'm some kind of a freak or somethin'."

"I remember that she was supposed to be involved in some sort of a scam."

"I heard that, too, but I don't believe it for a minute.

Do you know she'd sometimes call me 'Grandy'? Said I reminded her of her dead grandmother."

I had to bite my lip and dig my fingernails into my palm so I wouldn't react to that.

Regina shook her head sadly and wiped a tear from the corner of her eye with a plump forefinger. Then she reached into the sleeve of her dress and pulled out a lace-edged hankie and blew her nose.

"You said Timmy was no longer here. Do you know where he is?"

"He's got family over in Arcadia. He might have went there."

"I understand he dropped out of school at the end of last semester. Do you know why?"

"I kinda got the idea he decided art school weren't for him. I think he was trying to figure out what he did want to do. He talked some about going to Florida A&M, but it was too late to get in this year."

"So what has he been doing?"

"What so many kids do here—bein' a waiter. You make purty good tips during season. He worked up on the Trail somewheres."

Regina obviously was trying to be helpful, but she wasn't able to give me much concrete information. I was disappointed that Timothy wasn't here, but hoped I could find him in Arcadia. If I'd gone all the way to Miami looking for information, why not Arcadia? It was much closer. I didn't have much else to do with my time, and now that I'd jumped on this self-propelling ride, it was hard to get off. I hadn't forgotten Cal's admonition to be careful, but Timothy didn't sound threatening. Quite the opposite.

"I'll let myself out," I told Regina as I got ready to leave. I couldn't bear the thought of her trying to get up.

"Oh, no, no," she said, and she placed her hands on the arms of her chair and boosted herself slowly to her feet. It was painful to watch her struggle to gain her balance as she thrust herself away from the chair to a standing position.

She wiped her perspiring brow with the back of her hand. "I need the exercise," she said and gave a little laugh.

I walked slowly toward the porch with Regina following. I stood to one side to let her open the door. The least I could do was let her be the gracious hostess.

Outside, I turned to thank her.

"Somethin' you might want to know in case you find Timmy," she said before I had a chance to say anything. "I think he and Beth had a fight or somethin' not long before she drowned. I didn't see her here at the last. Maybe he blamed hisself for what happened to her. Anyways, he took it terrible hard. So you might want to be careful what you say to him. Be best if you not mention it at all, in fact."

I went to Publix to pick up the groceries I needed. But my mind was on Timothy Oldenburg. Regina said he might have blamed himself for Beth's death, presumably because they broke up. Perhaps he knew more than anyone else about the circumstances that drove her to participate in a scam. Could he have been involved? If not, I didn't want to add to his grief or his feelings of guilt. But I'd make that call when I met him.

I made a special effort to buy Mark's favorite foods, although his penchant for things with a high fat content worried me. But now was not the time to fuss about it. So I picked up frozen French fries, chocolate ice cream (he hated low-fat frozen yogurt or any other substitute), steaks and frozen pizza.

When I got home, Mark was fixing himself a brunch that probably added twenty points to his cholesterol count. The kitchen reeked with the odor of frying hash browns, scrambled eggs and bacon. Well, at least he'd given up smoking a couple of years ago. And I was delighted he had his appetite back.

"Got any more groceries in the car?" he asked as I dumped two bulging paper bags on the counter. This was the worst part of living on the eleventh floor. I had a cart I could use stored in the guest bedroom closet, but I inevitably forget to take it with me.

"Thanks, but this is it. I try to buy only what I can carry up on one trip. It means I shop more often, but when I'm alone I don't eat all that much."

I unloaded the bags and put away the food as Mark ate his meal with relish. His emotional ups and downs never affected his appetite for long.

When I finished, I sat down opposite him with a cup of coffee.

He looked at me curiously and then said, "Something's going on that you aren't telling me about."

Uh-oh. "What do you mean?"

"Detective Caronis called you. He wants you to call him back." Mark knew Caronis from a few months before when I got into so much trouble trying to find my friend Gerry's killer. There was no way I could pass it off as an overdue parking ticket.

I didn't say anything for a minute, trying to come up with a story that would placate him.

"Mom!" He wasn't going to let it slide.

"Oh, Mark. It's a sad story I didn't want to burden you with. I figured you had enough grief already. The girl who drowned was someone I knew casually, a very talented artist. I met her at Point of Rocks where she was painting a picture of Crescent Beach. That's why I didn't want to discuss it with that ditz on the beach, and why I wasn't completely truthful about it. I felt I couldn't bear to talk about it. Enough is enough."

"Okay, you have a point—I guess," he said, and I thought I was off the hook. "But that woman on the beach said something about a scam. What's that all about?"

"The media hasn't said much about it." I was being truthful; they really hadn't. Apparently the police were releasing very little information as long as the case was still open, even though their investigation seemed half-hearted at this point. "And she didn't seem like the kind who'd be involved in something like that," I added, which was also true.

"And that's all you know?"

I shrugged my shoulders and tried my damnedest to look innocent.

"Then why are you getting a call from the cops?"

"They couldn't identify her at first. But from the description I heard on TV, I thought it might be Beth. Unfortunately, I made the identification at the morgue. I pray I never have to do that again."

"No wonder you don't want to talk about it." He at last was showing some compassion. "So that's what the call's about?"

"I would assume so. Probably thanking me for my help."

"Did your Miami trip have something to do with all this? You sure have been closemouthed about it."

Good Lord, he was never going to let up. "I went to see her parents to give them my condolences."

"Uh-huh." He studied my face for a while. "You'd drive across the state to see them? And you knew this girl only casually."

"It was such a tragedy, Mark. I thought a visit in person was called for. And I guess I was thinking how I'd feel if something happened to you."

Mark had finished his breakfast and got up to rinse off his plate. "Okay, then, if that's your story, I guess I'll have to go along with it. But, frankly, Mom, it all sounds pretty flaky to me."

I tried my best to look outraged. "Well, that's a heck of a thing to say to your mother."

He stacked his dishes neatly in the dishwasher and then came over and put his arm around my shoulder and squeezed. "Ever since Dad died, you've held me at arm's length, never asking for help or letting me do anything for you. Look, I know you want to prove you can go it alone, but we all have to rely on each other sometimes. I know you manage very well. But damn it, that's what families are for, to be there in a pinch."

I reached up and patted his hand. "I love you, darling. And I know you'd do anything for me. Believe me, I'll ask for help if I ever need to."

Mark hung around the house for a while, and I knew he wanted to listen in when I returned Caronis's call. But I told him I had some letters to write and bills to pay that had to be ready before the mailman got there and immediately became engrossed in my checkbook. He finally gave up trying to outwait me and said he was going out on the beach. I called Detective Caronis as soon as he left.

"Mrs. Daniels, how are you?" He sounded relaxed and congenial.

"Fine. Did you find out something new?"

"A man standing on his seawall near where Beth's body was found saw a couple of packets wrapped in foil in a shallow place near shore. We think this could be part of the money you'd given her."

"How much was in them?" We'd divided it up into many small packages as instructed.

"One package had seven hundred and fifty dollars. The other package was nothing but cut-up magazine pages the size of bills. It was pretty well mush from being in the water so long in spite of the foil wrapping."

"So that was one of the packages she'd already wrapped before I got there."

"Seems that way. We'll have to keep your money for a while as evidence. But you'll get it back eventually."

"Think there's a chance of recovering more?"

"We checked the bottom over a pretty wide area near where it was found, but we came up empty. I wouldn't count on it."

"Anything else?" My hope that they'd uncover Beth's motive was fading day by day.

"No, that's it." My expectations went down another notch. "Thanks for returning my call. We'll keep in touch."

I hung up, hoping he wouldn't call me again until after Mark left.

I tried to figure out how I could go to Arcadia and look for Timothy as long as Mark was staying with me. Arcadia is about fifty miles due east of Sarasota on Route 70, so it takes an hour to get there. Then I'd have to find him once I arrived and, if I was lucky enough to do so, spend some time talking to him. In other words, I would need to devote a day to this. I knew I couldn't concoct a story for Mark about going shopping for the day or playing bridge that he would believe. He knew me too well for that.

While I was considering all this, the phone rang. A familiar voice said, "Hi, it's me."

"Hi, Cal."

"I was wondering if the three of us could do something together."

That was the last thing I wanted to do. It would double the chance that either Cal or I would accidentally spill the beans. But it did give me an idea.

"I have a better suggestion. I want to go to Arcadia, and I'd like to tell Mark you need to go there to do research for a travel article. I don't want him along."

"Why Arcadia?"

"I'll explain that tomorrow."

"Well, okay. What time?"

"Oh, about ten."

"Great. I'll see you then."

Mark probably wouldn't be too happy I was going off again, but I planned to tell him that since he spent most of his time on the beach, I burn too easily to be with him. And he surely couldn't expect me to sit around twiddling my thumbs just because he was in town.

FIFTEEN

I WAITED UNTIL SUPPER to tell Mark I was going to Arcadia. I'd cooked a pork roast and sweet potatoes, his dad's favorite dinner, which was kind of underhanded, and was perversely pleased when he said, "Great meal. Dad would have loved this."

"Hon," I said, my stomach churning but my smile plastered on, "I almost forgot. Cal wants me to go to Arcadia with him tomorrow. He's doing research for a travel article."

"What's so interesting about Arcadia?" Was he trying to trip me up?

Thankfully there'd been an article in the paper just a couple of weeks earlier on the town, so I could speak with some authority.

"It has a rather charming historic district and is typical of old Florida towns. Almost the entire business district, forty-three buildings, burnt to the ground in 1905 from a fire that started in a livery stable. Only three buildings were left."

"I assume it's been rebuilt."

"Oh, sure. But of course those buildings are now over a century old."

We were settling down to watch one of the sappier

sitcoms, which I never watch when I'm alone, when there was a knock at the door.

I opened it to find Jean Jacobs looking as sad as I've ever seen her. Jean normally is the perkiest person I've ever known, and her perkiness is genuine and delightful, a rare characteristic. This was totally unlike her.

"Come in, Jean," I said, worried.

Mark turned off the TV and stood to greet her.

"I hope I'm not intruding," she said anxiously.

"Of course not. Come on, sit down."

She settled on one end of the couch, and I sat on the other.

Mark looked a bit uncomfortable. "Would you two like to be alone? I can go out on the beach."

"Oh, of course not," Jean said, waving for him to be seated. "It's dark out there."

"Is something the matter, Jean?" I asked, stating the obvious.

"Ross isn't home, and I just got some bad news. I guess I needed someone's shoulder to cry on."

"What on earth?" I was afraid there'd been a death in the family.

"My son, Sam, and his wife, Barb, are breaking up." She had a tissue in her hand and she wiped her eyes.

I sneaked a look at Mark. His eyes were averted and he was biting his upper lip. His marriage was still on very rocky ground in spite of Cindy's promise to get professional help. This was just too close to home for him.

"I'm so sorry, Jean."

"I'll have to admit I'm not all that sorry about losing her as a daughter-in-law. Frankly, there was little love lost between us. It's just that Sam is so crazy about her. It's really hurt him."

"You're saying it's her idea?" I hated that this conversation was going on in front of Mark, but he would at least know that others were in as much pain as he was. I know Jean would have been mortified had she known what Mark and Cindy had been going through.

"Yes, and she really won't give him a good reason. Something about being bored with him." Now, that was cruel. At least Cindy hadn't said that to Mark, as far as I knew, anyway. I don't know which would be harder to take, unfaithfulness or being told how boring you are.

We talked another fifteen or twenty minutes. I was so afraid Jean would ask Mark his opinion about it, but she didn't. In fact, I have a suspicion that his unusually solemn demeanor might have made her cut her visit short. At any rate she finally said, "Well, I've got to make some phone calls. Thanks for being my crying post, Emma."

When I shut the door after Jean, I turned to find Mark with tears in his eyes. "I really hope Cindy and I can make it this time," he finally said. "Why the hell do we have so much trouble working it out?"

"Sometimes people, even with the best of intentions, just can't make a go of it."

"When she left me the first time, it damn near killed me. But at least there seemed to be a reason for it. She

taken in the fifties when only a couple of roads and a handful of cottages scattered here and there showed any sign of habitation. The rest was covered with jungle-like growth. The main thing I love about Siesta Key is that, unlike other Florida islands, much of that natural growth still exists throughout the neighborhoods east of the village and from the Stickney Point Bridge south. But north of the bridge, a virtual wall of multistory condominiums along Midnight Pass obscures the view of the Gulf unless you happen to live in one. You know what they say: now that I'm here, build a ditch across the top of Florida and don't let anyone else in.

I picked up a four-pack of water and a six-pack of beer, placed them on the backseat floor and drove back toward La Hacienda. Cal wasn't coming to pick me up for another two hours, so I hoped to get an hour or so in walking on the beach before he came.

I was about two blocks away from my parking lot, when suddenly my steering wheel just quit working. I noticed the car had started to drift toward the left, and when I tried to steer to the right, nothing happened. It was like being on a road and hitting black ice and losing complete control in a matter of seconds. I'll admit I was going a little faster than the speed limit, but there was so little traffic, and I was anxious to get home and out on the beach.

Before I fully realized what was happening and could stomp on my brakes, the car went across the road, over a sidewalk and into the concrete wall surrounding the parking lot of a condominium building with a loud thud.

My car is too old to have air bags, but it has seat belts, which I've used without fail since a friend was killed because she'd neglected to use hers. I was temporarily thrown up and forward slightly, and my head just glanced off the rearview mirror. I was in such a state of shock for a minute, I just sat there without moving. It was past tourist season and early in the day, so no one was around. I finally stumbled out of the car, checked myself over and seemed to be in one piece except for a smallish lump on my forehead. I gingerly walked around to the front of my car to assess the damage. Though I feared I had sustained some major damage from the sound of the impact, it hadn't been as bad as I thought. The left front headlight was smashed, the bumper didn't look in very good shape, but all in all, I had been extremely lucky. It could have been so very much worse. Apparently I'd been able to at least tap the brakes enough, and some low-lying plants at the edge of the road had slowed down the car's momentum.

A Lexus appeared in the northbound lane going toward the village. It pulled off to the side of the road next to me, and a young woman got out. She ran over to me.

"Are you okay?" She was dressed in a beach cover-up and was probably on her way to nearby Siesta Beach.

"Yeah, I'm all right," I said. "A little shook up, but everything seems to work. On my body, that is, not my car. Something happened to my steering."

She pulled a cell phone out of her pocket. "I'm calling 9-1-1."

I was glad she did. I was still pretty rattled.

In about ten minutes a patrol car pulled up and a young patrolman got out. He wore shades and had a trim mustache that he probably grew to make himself look more mature. He asked the same thing the woman had. "Are you okay?"

I assured him I was. He walked around to the front of my car. "Looks like it's drivable."

"'Fraid not," I told him. "My steering went out. I couldn't hold it on the road."

"Okay, I'll call a tow truck. Then we can fill out the forms."

I thanked the woman in the Lexus, and she drove away. The cop and I got through all the paperwork by the time the tow truck got there. I watched with considerable sadness as my Civic was taken away. It had been such a good little car, and I prayed it could be fixed and I could drive it another ten years.

"Can I take you home?" the cop asked.

"No, that's okay. I live just a couple of blocks from here. I can walk, but thanks anyway." I had retrieved the beer and water from the backseat, so with a pack in each hand I started to trudge toward La Hacienda. I began to suspect very soon that I should have accepted the ride, since I forgot how heavy multiple bottles can be. By the time I'd reached the drive, I wished I'd left them in the car.

On the way up in the elevator, I mulled over what I would tell Mark. He was going to find out sooner or later, so there was no use in postponing the inevitable.

He was sitting on the balcony reading the paper by

the time I got home. I put the beer and water in the refrigerator and walked out to join him.

"Where you been, Ma?" he asked.

"Went to get you some beer. I'd forgotten it when I went shopping."

He smiled. "You didn't need to do that. I could have gotten my own."

"I wanted some bottled water to take with us to Arcadia."

"Oh, okay. Thanks for the beer," he said and went back to reading the comics.

"Mark," I said hesitantly, "I had a little problem on the way home."

He looked up at me, suspicion in his eyes. "When you say 'little,' that always rings alarm bells. What kind of problem?"

"My steering went out on the way back. I hit a wall."

He threw the paper down. "Oh, my God, are you okay?"

"I bumped my head on the rearview mirror. I guess I should put ice on it."

"Where's the car?"

"It's been towed. There wasn't too much damage, Mark. The left headlight is smashed and the bumper has to be replaced, but I was lucky."

He still looked dismayed. "Have you had it serviced lately? After all, it is pretty old."

I tried to think when I'd last had it to the garage. "I guess it was five or six months ago."

"You need to have it checked more regularly. In fact, you need to buy a new car. One with air bags."

"I love that car, Mark. It's done very well by me. Besides, I can't afford a new one just now." Of course, if I hadn't just lost a small fortune to Beth, I could very well have bought one. Not that I was ready to trade in my fun little hatchback.

"Then let me help you buy one."

I shook my head vigorously. "No way, Mark. I'll not let you support me. Besides, with Cindy in treatment, you could have some big medical bills."

His eyes betrayed the fact he hadn't thought about that. He grimaced and shook his head. "How are you getting to Arcadia?"

"Cal planned to drive."

"Well, when you get home, you can use my car if you need it. I'm not going anywhere but the beach. Do you know when you might get yours back?"

"Don't have a clue. And the garage wouldn't know yet. I'll call them this afternoon. In the meantime I'm going out on the beach for a while. I need a little downtime."

"Okay, Ma. Just please be careful."

"Why? Do you think a shark is going to get me?" A little humor can sometimes defuse a situation.

He gave me a halfhearted smile and picked up his newspaper.

I went to the kitchen and made an ice pack out of a large Ziploc bag, grabbed a beach towel out of the linen

closet and headed for the beach. I wasn't even going
to take the time to put on shorts. I didn't want a tan. I
wanted peace and quiet.

SIXTEEN

THE ICE PACK MADE THE lump on my forehead go away, so I didn't tell Cal about my eventful morning until we were out of Sarasota. I was afraid he'd want to cancel our plans. He'd called me from his car as he waited at the front entrance, so he didn't notice that my car was missing from my designated parking space. Besides, with Mark's car in the visitor's spot next to mine, there had been nowhere for Cal to park except at the far edge of the lot. The gentleman that he is, he thinks he needs to come to my door to get me, but I'd told him that was a waste of time. I wasn't hung up on old-fashioned manners.

When I finally got up the nerve to confess to my accident, Cal started to pull the car off the road, but there was nowhere to park with a drainage ditch alongside the berm.

"You're sure you're all right?" he asked, taking his eyes off the pavement long enough to give me a once-over.

"Of course. Otherwise I wouldn't be here."

"What do you think happened?"

I shrugged. "It's an old car, Cal. I guess I need to have it checked over more often."

"What are you going to drive while it's being fixed?"

"Mark said I could use his."

I wanted to steer him away from the subject, so I told him about Cindy showing up.

"What a fiasco. Why does he put up with it?"

"He claims he loves her so much he's desperate to make a go of it."

"Sometimes you've just got to let go," he said. I knew he was thinking about his ex who dumped him after many years of marriage.

"Then Jean came over last night and said Sam and Barb are breaking up. Of course, she had no idea of Mark's situation as she was telling us this."

"So Sam finally came to his senses and dumped Barb?"

"No, she left him. Said he bored her."

"I could never understand his attraction to Barb. Frankly, I think he's damn lucky to be rid of her."

"Well, I guess he doesn't feel that way. Jean says he's devastated."

"Men can be such damn fools." I'm sure he was talking about Mark as much as Sam. And I had to agree with him.

The day was overcast and humid, but no rain was forecast.

"So what's in Arcadia?" Cal asked. "Knowing you, it must have something to do with Beth."

"I checked on Timothy Oldenburg through a teacher at Ringling School. He gave me his last address in town, but he'd moved out right after Beth died. His landlady told me his family lives in Arcadia."

"You've been a busy little bee."

"Well...I couldn't leave that loose end dangling. I'd like to talk to him."

"Emma, did it ever occur to you that you might get yourself in trouble if you keep digging away?"

I waved the notion away. "You'll be with me. It's the middle of the day, and he doesn't know we're coming. What could possibly happen? Besides, he sounds positively wholesome."

"So did Beth," he replied darkly.

"Well, Cal, you surprise me. You weren't uptight about going to Miami. Why now?"

"I didn't expect you to be so dogged about this. I thought you'd talk to her parents and that would be that."

"They left me with more questions than answers. I still don't know what drove Beth, but damn it, I intend to find out. I think you're overreacting to the danger part. I haven't met any hardened criminals yet." I meant it as a joke, but Cal was having none of it.

"You said that the last time. And it nearly got you killed."

I didn't have an answer to that one.

We had driven out Stickney Point Road to Clark Road and out of the city. Once we were past I-75, the developments eventually thinned out and we were into the countryside—flat, grassy land dotted with slash pine and palmetto. A few more miles out we passed Myakka

Park—a wooded oasis of sabal palms, live oak, pines and maple trees.

I thought again how Beth had told me she was going to meet the kidnappers at Myakka Park but ended up in a boat on the Gulf. I assumed she wanted to mislead me in case I decided to call the cops, probably wanting them to go as far east as possible while she headed north along the coast.

For the rest of the drive we said little. Cal played an Aaron Neville CD, the sort of thoughtful gesture he made frequently. I'd once told him that I was a fan of his.

It took a little over an hour, through miles of incredibly flat land with no sign of development. Closer to Arcadia we began to pass fields of grazing cattle and acres of orange groves. A huge orange-processing plant towered over the land just west of town.

When we arrived in Arcadia, I began looking around for the effects of Hurricane Charley that had devastated the little town in 2004. I could find little to indicate the wrath of the storm. Time heals and life goes on.

When we arrived at the intersection of Highways 72 and 70, we began looking for an outdoor telephone. Cal had a cell phone but we needed a local phone directory. We'd crossed to the east side of town and were nearly out in the country again when we found a strip shopping center that had a pay phone in front of the Dollar Store, a true relic of the past. When I went up to it, I realized that the receiver had been pulled out of the phone, so it was there only because nobody had yet carted it away.

At least there was still a directory stashed underneath the little shelf, probably out-of-date but perhaps still helpful.

I looked in the slender directory and found two Oldenburgs, Harvey Q. and Roger A. I wondered what the *Q* was for and the only thing I could think of was Quentin. I wrote the numbers down and got back in the car to use Cal's phone.

I dialed Harvey's residence first. An older woman answered.

"May I speak to Timothy please?" I asked.

"You've got the wrong Oldenburg," she said. "That would be Roger's son."

I thanked her and hung up. "Wrong Oldenburg," I told Cal. "Should I call first or just go over there?"

"He might not feel like talking, so why give him warning? Let's go on to the house."

I'd written both addresses down. "It's on South Hillsboro. I remember crossing that when we came through town."

We retraced our steps, found Hillsboro and turned left, reasoning their street number would be in that direction. We found the small frame bungalow two blocks away, its tin roof typical of early-twentieth-century houses. In fact, Arcadia seems to be a town of wooden bungalows from the early part of the century, much different from the stucco ranches and newer two-story homes that make up so much of Sarasota. But that's because Sarasota's growth came mostly from the fifties on.

The fat brick pillars that supported the porch on the Oldenburg home had been painted a bright blue, along with the window trim, bringing an unexpected touch of color to a street of plain white houses. A large bottle-brush tree shaded the front yard, and hibiscus bloomed colorfully along the lot line.

After pulling up in front, Cal said, "Do you have some sort of cover story? Or is frankness the order of the day?"

"I'll play it as it lies."

"Do you want me to come with you?" he asked.

"Would you mind if I went alone? I don't want him to feel he's outnumbered."

"Whatever you say." There was a tiny bit of impatience in his voice. I had a hunch that my preoccupation with Beth was wearing a bit thin with Cal.

I went to the door and knocked several times, but no one answered. Even though it was a fine day with a light breeze, the windows were all shut and the venetian blinds closed. Either no one was home or they were reclusive.

I was crossing the lawn, feeling frustrated and regretting that I'd made Cal bring me on this wild-goose chase, when a middle-aged woman dressed in flowered Capri pants and a striped blouse came around from behind the house next-door. She wore gardening gloves and carried a pair of hedge clippers and began to trim the bushes beside her front door.

Approaching her, I asked, "Excuse me. Do the Oldenburgs live next door?"

She smiled pleasantly. "Yes, they do."

"Is Timothy living at home now?"

"Yes." She nodded. "He moved back home this week, as a matter of fact."

"Do you have any idea where I might find him?"

I could tell she was consumed with curiosity but too polite to ask. "He's working at Sam's Service Station. It's on South Brevard. That's Route 17."

I thanked her and returned to the car. I could see her in the outside mirror watching us as we drove away. I was relieved I didn't yet have to tell Cal that our trip here was fruitless.

Sam's was on the southern edge of town, an old gas station that was full service, a rarity in this day and age. There was no large convenience store loaded with calorie-packed munchies, no brightly colored pumps that let you charge your gas directly to your credit card. Just a small two-bay garage with a tiny, dingy office where only motor oil was sold, and a beat-up soft-drink machine against the outside wall where you could get a Coke for fifty-five cents. Two ancient pumps dispensed gas. There were no buttons to push to select the grade. You took what they offered.

There were no other cars when Cal pulled in and parked next to the building. As I was opening the car door, a good-looking young man came out of the office. He was about Beth's age, had blond hair that looked as though it had been bleached in the sun, deep blue eyes, and was what young people would refer to as a hunk.

"May I help you, ma'am?"

"Are you Timothy Oldenburg?"

"Why, yes, ma'am."

I could tell he wondered how I knew his name. I'd expected a "Who the hell wants to know?" which seems more common these days than the polite obsequiousness of this young man. I wondered if it was his "on duty" persona or if he was always this charming.

"I'd like to talk to you for a few minutes if that's possible."

"As long as I'm not busy with customers. Want to go in the office?" He didn't seem particularly curious about my request. But then he probably never suspected someone would come from Sarasota to talk to him about his former girlfriend.

The office didn't look too appealing, but there was nowhere else to go for a private conversation, so I nodded yes. Once we were inside, he pushed a beat-up chair away from the desk on its squeaking rollers and motioned me to sit down, after wiping off the seat with a clean rag. Its torn green vinyl upholstery was sticky and hot, and I could feel the sharp edges of the torn cover through my slacks. He then perched on the corner of the scratched metal desk.

He was looking at me quizzically, waiting for me to begin, so I took a deep breath and plunged in.

"My name is Emma Daniels, and I was a friend of Beth Wilkinson's," I began and watched his face drain of color. I hurried on before I lost my resolve. "I'm having trouble accepting the circumstances of her death. The reason I've come to you is that I'm hoping you can cast some light on what happened. I can't believe what they're saying about her."

Timothy looked physically ill. "I can't talk about it." He hung his head and wouldn't look at me, hoping, I think, that I would just go away.

"Look, I know how you feel," I said. "I lost my husband recently. It's the hardest thing I ever had to go through."

He looked up and nodded his head mutely; he was in such obvious pain.

"I would find it even harder to endure," I continued, "if he died doing something wrong, something uncharacteristic of him."

He studied my face, clearly wondering where I was going with this.

"If my husband were accused of doing something illegal, I would do everything to get to the bottom of it. I would never accept it. That's the way I feel about Beth, too."

He took a handkerchief out of his pocket and wiped perspiration from his face, though I think a few tears were poised to erupt, as well. He just didn't want me to know it. "So what are you saying?"

"I'm trying to find a reason, a motive for her to get involved in a scam. Everyone I've talked to has been shocked by it. They say it's so unlike her. There had to be a very compelling reason."

Timothy's face reflected infinite sadness. "You're right, because the Beth I knew would never do anything like that. The trouble is I have no idea what could have prompted her to do it."

"Would you be willing to answer some questions for me?"

He inspected his oil-grimed fingernails as he thought about it. "Depends on what you ask, I guess."

"How do you feel about what I'm doing? Don't you want to know what made her do it?"

This time he chewed on his lower lip. I could see he was torn between not wanting to talk about her because it was so painful, and being intrigued by my quest. "Don't think I haven't asked myself that a thousand times."

"Well, maybe between the two of us we can come up with something."

He exhaled a deep sigh. "Okay."

"I talked with your landlady, Regina…"

Tim's eyes grew large. "You're kidding."

"No, Tim, I'm not kidding. I'm very serious about this. She says that you and Beth broke up a while back. Is that true?"

He looked at me in disbelief. "I never told her that."

"No, but Beth hadn't been around for a while. She was very fond of her, you know. It wasn't hard to figure out that you two had split."

He covered his eyes with his hands and rocked back and forth in distress. "It was Beth's doing. Not mine." He paused. "I loved her." His voice cracked on "loved."

I was beginning to feel pretty rotten now. Tim had endured the heartbreak of both rejection and death. That's a lot to go through, particularly for one so young.

His arms fell limply into his lap, and I reached over and squeezed his hand. "I'm so sorry to dredge this all up. I know how painful it is. But I can't help feeling there's some connection. Some cause and effect."

"How could there be?"

"Because the only other reason that's conceivable for her needing so much money was to finance her education. And her mother told me she was going to ask an uncle to help with the tuition."

"Yes, she told me he was going to help her out."

"So that's why I'm here. I came over here on the slim chance you'd help me discover Beth's motive."

"What can I tell you?"

I looked him straight in the eye. "You can tell me why you broke up."

"Oh, God," he said. Finally, his voice so low I could barely hear him, he began to talk. "We loved each other so much. I hoped that one day we could marry. But Beth was intent on finishing her education first. Her folks wouldn't help her out—her dad's a real tyrant—but she was willing to take off a semester now and then to earn enough money for tuition. This was before her mother offered to help her."

I nodded as I already knew all that.

"The problem is she got pregnant." He waited for my reaction, but when I showed none, he continued. "I was upset because I wasn't in a position to support a family. I'd already discovered that art school wasn't for me. I simply don't have enough talent. I wanted to go to Tallahassee to engineering school, but I also needed to earn money for tuition. If I got married and started a family, I'd never be able to go on to school, and I'd probably end up doing something like this for the rest of my life." His eyes swept the room, and he grimaced as if the mere thought of it was appalling. "I told Beth I loved her and wanted to marry her when I got out of school, but I couldn't deal with a baby now."

"How did she react?"

"She seemed very stoic about it. At least to me. Now, in hindsight, I'm sure she was only pretending to take it in stride."

"Did she have an abortion?"

"Yes." His voice almost faded away, and he looked ashamed. "And after that, she wouldn't see me anymore." I thought he was going to break down, but he didn't. "God, I thought she was as much in favor of it as I was."

"With her upbringing, I imagine it was an extremely difficult thing for her to do."

"But she'd rejected most of her parents' ideas. She told me that she couldn't wait to get away from their narrow-minded dogma. As far as they were concerned, damn near everything was a sin."

"I'm sure she didn't tell them about the abortion, though."

"Oh, jeez, no. She didn't agree with them, but she

sure didn't intend to buck them, either. She just hoped she could quietly live her life the way she wanted, away from their influence. Her philosophy was what they didn't know didn't hurt them, or, more important, wouldn't hurt her. I think she was a little bit afraid of them, her dad especially."

I wondered briefly if she'd taken my money to pay for her abortion. But that idea was ridiculous. No abortion cost more than a fraction of the money I gave her. And apparently she'd had the procedure some weeks earlier.

"Did you pay for the abortion?"

"I didn't have enough money at the time. I was a waiter, and the tips weren't all that great the past few months. So I asked my former roommate for a loan. We shared a dorm room when I was still on campus. His parents paid his way and gave him a generous allowance."

"Why did you leave the dorm and move to Regina's?"

"I didn't like Jimmy Dale's lifestyle. He smoked pot all the time, and I thought it was pretty childish behavior. He was a party boy and had people in our room day and night. Couldn't get any sleep or study there."

"Jimmy Dale who?"

"Hippert."

"Is he still at Ringling?"

"I think so. Why do you want to know about him?"

"Trying to cover all the bases. At this point, I've no idea what's significant and what's not."

A car pulled up to one of the two gas pumps, rumbling noisily through a faulty muffler, though the engine noise was outclassed by the radio turned on full blast. It was country music, something peppy by Carrie Underwood.

"Excuse me a minute." Timothy slid off the desk and went outside to pump gas. I glanced at Cal's car and saw he was reading a paperback. Must have brought it along, suspecting I might leave him twiddling his thumbs somewhere. Poor Cal. I'd taken advantage of him almost from the moment I met him. He must be sick of my compulsive snooping, I thought. No way to build a relationship. But then he was still around.

I watched as Tim washed the windshield and checked under the hood. That was a service hard to come by anymore. It made me darn near nostalgic. Finally the driver left, and he returned to the office.

"Sorry," he said, slumping back down onto the desk.

"Can you tell me about Jimmy Dale? I was kind of wondering about him. How could he afford to loan you money?"

Tim shrugged. "His family sends it to him, I think. That's the impression I've always had. You know, though, he never talked about them much. I don't think they were exactly estranged—I just don't think he gave much of a damn about them. Pretty self-centered guy. I didn't like him much, but he was the only one I knew who could loan me what I needed."

"How did you pay him back?"

"I purely worked my tail off, working extra shifts

whenever they'd let me, and finally got enough together to pay him off. By that time, Beth wouldn't have anything to do with me. When she died, I couldn't bear to stay in Sarasota, so I came back home and got this job."

"Are you going back to school?"

He shook his head dejectedly. "I don't know. I'm so damn depressed right now, I really don't care anymore."

I wondered if the whole world was in a depressive state. Sometimes I got the impression all young people were going through traumas we rarely encountered when we were their age. Not only was the business of making a living more fraught with pitfalls and detours and stress, their personal relationships were nothing but roller-coaster rides, with the lows outweighing the highs. I felt sorry for the whole damned generation. As a mother, I wished there was something I could do to make it better.

"Look, Tim," I said, "I'm sorry to put you through this. If I find out anything that would explain what Beth did, you'll be the first to know. I realize it's not going to change the outcome, but at least we'll understand her a little better."

He nodded, but his body language betrayed total despair. He said nothing.

"I wish you luck," I said, getting up.

He didn't move from the desk as I went out to the car. When Cal pulled away from the station, I saw Tim wipe his eyes with the now-greasy hankie that he'd stuck in his hip pocket.

SEVENTEEN

"REMEMBER THE DeSOTO Restaurant we passed on the way into town?" I asked Cal.

"Not really."

"It's just a half block west on Route 70. May I buy you lunch there? They have home cooking."

"Is this a bribe?"

"What?" I turned and looked at him. He was grinning.

"You think I'm pissed for having to sit in the car so long, and you're tying to make amends. Right?"

Well, damn him. No chance at all to be sneaky with this guy. "Well…"

"I accept your apology and, yes, I'm hungry."

What could I say after that? I'd been preempted.

The DeSoto is across the street from the restored train station, the centerpiece of downtown Arcadia. The restaurant had once been the dining room for a hotel, but the hotel is empty now, its painted brick facade peeling and shabby. The clue that the two had been connected was revealed when I used the restroom. I had to go through a small, empty lobby that contains only an L-shaped registration desk layered with dust and grime. Still taped to its top are hand-lettered signs saying Rent

Must be Paid On Time and No Pets Allowed. Access to the stairs is barred by a wire grill. It seemed so far removed from the teeming, elegant buildings of Sarasota, I could almost feel the spirits lingering here, remnants of a Florida long forgotten.

It was nearly twelve-thirty now and the dining room was nearly full, but we managed to find a table in the corner. Cal ordered fried chicken breast with yellow rice, and I ordered chef salad. I knew their full meals were good, as well as inexpensive, but if I ate that much at noon, I'd be a goner for the rest of the day. My stomach seems to be connected to my sleep center, and too much food fills me with inertia.

I repeated my conversation with Tim, as close to word for word as I could remember.

"So what's the game plan now?"

"To be honest, I don't know. The only new name I've got is Jimmy Dale Hippert. And all he did was loan Tim the money for the abortion. If Tim hadn't been able to pay him back, I'd probably want to talk to him. But the loan was paid off, so there doesn't seem to be much point. Besides, he doesn't sound like a very pleasant character."

"Hmm." I didn't know if Cal was commenting about Jimmy Dale or enjoying his chicken.

After we finished our meal, we decided to drive back to Myakka Park and spend a couple of hours. Cal's quite interested in birding, but I'm strictly an amateur. I've always enjoyed watching the birds, particularly since they are so different in Florida from the ones I was familiar with in Ohio, but I'm not good at identifying them. Cal keeps binoculars and a bird book in his car at all times and keeps a log of each new bird he identifies.

We drove the winding road into the center of Myakka and parked next to a thick grove of huge live oaks heavily draped in Spanish moss. We explored this area first. Their branches teemed with turkey vultures that would take off and soar in dizzying circles, floating on air currents. Sometimes the sky would be filled with dozens of them, each tracing his own circular path so that from a distance they resembled a swarm of drunken mosquitoes. Cal pointed out red-tailed hawks, egrets, ibis and heron as we came out on the edge of Myakka Lake, and he was delighted when he saw two Sandhill cranes, the first he'd spotted at the park. We took a ride in the airboat, the world's largest, designed to sail above the water hyacinths that have proliferated in its waters and would quickly snarl a propeller. Dozens of alligators stretched out in the sun along the muddy banks or swam smoothly and silently like resurrected Mesozoic creatures in a theme park.

It was late afternoon before we returned to Siesta Key. As we pulled into the parking lot, I said, "Want to come up? I can fix turkey sandwiches and soup for supper."

"No. Thanks, anyway," Cal replied. "As long as Mark is here, I think he would prefer to have you to himself while he's going through this crisis."

"I just hope his crisis isn't compounded by this Beth thing. If he finds out the whole story, he'll be all over my case and start pestering the police. That's the last thing I want."

"I can sympathize with that." Cal laughed. "It drives me nuts when my kids try to 'take care of Dad.'"

"Yours, too?"

"Oh, hell, what kids don't? They think we've reached our dotage at sixty."

"I'm not quite there yet."

"You're probably suffering from 'early onset of decrepitude.'"

I had to laugh, too. "My God, Cal, I don't think I'm quite ready for a nursing home yet."

"Me neither. We just have to work around the younger generation, that's all."

Mark was sitting on the balcony when I let myself into the condo.

"Hi, hon," I said, going out through the sliding glass door. "Have a nice day?"

"Sure. Very peaceful. Spent most of it on the beach. You have a good time?"

"It was okay," I answered, trying to be noncommittal.

"Could I take you out to dinner tonight?"

I'd eaten a huge salad for lunch, and I was really too full to eat much, but I didn't want to disappoint him again. "Sure, that would be nice."

Before we left, I called the garage where my car had been towed. I was hoping it could be fixed in the next few days before Mark went home. Otherwise I was going to have to get a rental.

"It's a wonder you weren't hurt badly," the manager told me. "The mechanic tells me that your tie rods were loose. That's why you lost control of the steering."

"What would cause that?" I asked. I had no idea what a tie rod was.

"Do you get your car checked over regularly?"

I was embarrassed to answer. "I guess I wait until something goes bad," I admitted. Paul had always maintained the car, and I never gave regular checkups much of a thought.

"This could just happen on an older car that wasn't well maintained, but I'd say it's more likely somebody tampered with it. If I were you, I think I'd talk to the cops and tell them what I said. Or do you want me to report it? I don't have concrete evidence, just a hunch."

Oh, my God! Could that be true? Why would anyone do such a thing? I wondered. "So you can't say for sure," I said.

"No, ma'am."

"Maybe I should talk to them. Can you tell me when my car might be fixed?"

"Should be ready by Friday. Had to send out for a headlight. Old model. Don't keep 'em on hand."

I hung up and sat there, stunned. I assumed that if my car had been tampered with, it had to be connected to Beth. How would anyone know that I'd been looking into her death? Other than her family and ex-boyfriend, and I didn't think they'd want to hurt me. At first I pulled a blank, and then I remembered the phone number on the slip of paper I'd found at the house on Casey Key. I'd called that number, and when the person at the other end hung up on me, Cal reminded me they probably had caller ID.

There was no way I was going to share this news with Mark. Cal was another story. I'd have to think about that. And should I call Caronis when I could do so in private? It was probably too late to reach him at work today. I decided I'd do it in the morning.

Mark and I watched the news before leaving for the restaurant. By ten after seven we pulled out of our parking lot and headed for the Trail. We were going to the Galleon, one of the grander seafood restaurants in the area, where tables are draped with pristine white tablecloths, the waiters are obsequious and soft lights give it a certain cachet. Paul and I usually went to a seafood place which featured a cavernous room filled with rows of rustic booths. There, each Formica table is equipped with plastic bottles of ketchup, tartar sauce and little baskets of sugar-substitute packets. But the fish is delicious and half the price.

The parking lot was nearly full, but he found a spot behind the restaurant at the far end of the lot. I got out and had started toward the building when Mark shouted, "Mom, look out!" I instinctively ran between the nearest cars, when a large black sedan went flashing by, missing me by inches. If Mark hadn't yelled, I'm sure it would have run over me. It was as though it had materialized out of thin air. I put my hand on the car beside me to steady myself; I was thoroughly shaken.

Mark ran over to me. "Are you okay?"

I didn't want him to know how alarmed I was. "Damn fool," I said. "Why do people drive like idiots in parking lots?"

"I could have sworn he was aiming right at you. He came around the corner like a bat out of hell."

"Don't be silly, Mark. He probably had too many drinks." I only wished I really believed that. Two incidents in one day didn't add up to coincidence. But I was determined we were going to have a pleasant, non-stressful dinner together. "Let's go stuff ourselves," I said, putting my arm through his, and we strolled into the restaurant as if nothing had happened. I prayed that my acting ability wouldn't fail me tonight, because I was still shaking on the inside, and I didn't think that feeling was going to dissipate anytime soon.

"Now, this is living," Mark said as the waiter placed a huge platter of food in front of him. We should have done this sooner. His spirits seemed higher than they'd been since he arrived.

Mark tore into his lobster-and-shrimp dinner, while I picked at mine. There was nothing wrong with it; I just wasn't hungry for more reasons than having eaten too much in Arcadia. He ended up finishing off my plate, too.

"Are you okay?" he asked, eyeing me worriedly as he ate the last of the sugar pea pods from my plate.

"Oh, sure," I lied. "I hadn't realized how full I still was from lunch. I don't know why restaurants make such huge servings. They are intent upon fattening up the world."

"I'm not complaining," he said as he patted his stomach.

I couldn't believe it when he ordered dessert. One would think I'd been starving him since he'd arrived.

"Oh, gosh, I forgot," he said as he dug into a chocolate brownie topped with ice cream, nuts, whipped topping and a cherry that made me almost gag to look at it. "Mrs. Jacobs called while you were gone. Said to give her a call back sometime. Nothing urgent."

"Oh, okay." Something further about Sam and Barb, no doubt. Frankly, I was getting a bit bored with hearing about her daughter-in-law. But she'd listened patiently to me many times when I'd talk about Paul. I felt I owed her.

It wasn't long after we returned home that the phone rang. I went out in the kitchen to answer it so I wouldn't disturb Mark's TV program. It was Cal.

"I got to thinking about your conversation with Timothy Oldenburg this afternoon," he said.

"Oh?"

"Well, yeah, he seemed to wrap everything up in a neat little package. But what if it was all bullshit? What if it was a story he made up to cover up his part in the swindle?"

"He seemed so sincere, though."

"So? What about Beth? Ms. Sincere herself."

He got me there. "What do you suggest?"

"The only one who can verify his story seems to be Jimmy Dale Hippert. Maybe you need to check it out with him."

"Cal, I can't believe it. You seem to be getting into the spirit of this. And I thought you were merely resigned to my involvement."

"It's kind of contagious, you know? Just make damn sure to be careful. Talk to him in the daylight and don't go in his house or anything."

I laughed. "So you got bit by the bug. Well, let me see if I can find him. I'll let you know what he says." For about two seconds I contemplated telling him about the call to the garage and the incident in the parking lot, but then I thought better of it. He'd surely change his mind about my talking to Jimmy Dale.

Mark raised an eyebrow when I came back to the living room, but I ignored his unspoken question and pretended to be completely absorbed in the cop show he was watching.

THE NEXT MORNING I TRIED to call Jean, but no one was home. I was relieved that I didn't have to hear a litany of sad tales about how awful Barb was. I know I cried on her shoulder sometimes, but I always thought my son's private life was nobody else's business, and I didn't discuss it with her.

It was Wednesday and time for my hair appointment. I don't spend hours getting perms and dye jobs; life's too short for that. Sometimes I think my femininity genes went awry somewhere along the line. I get a monthly shampoo, trim and blow-dry which takes forty-five minutes at most. But Mark didn't know that. He was used to Cindy spending several hours at the beauty parlor. When I left the house, Mark had just gotten up, and I told him I was getting my hair done and it might be a while before I got home. I knew he wouldn't think a thing of it.

As soon as I left Leona's Style Shop, I drove over to Ringling School. I waited till class break and went to Emile Szostak's classroom.

"Hello," he said when he saw me. "Mrs.... Mrs.... Daniels. Right?" He was wearing pretty much the same outfit as before, and he was taping some quick sketches of nudes drawn on newsprint up on the wall. Each picture consisted of only a few quick strokes. But it was pretty amazing how well the students could capture the human form in those few lines. He saw me studying them.

"I give them three minutes per pose. It loosens them up."

"That must be hard." I couldn't imagine how they could draw a complete body in that time.

"It's like anything else. The more practice the better. They tend to be too constrained otherwise. The body is very fluid."

"You talk like a dance teacher."

"We have a lot in common. Movement and grace are important in both art and dance."

I spent a couple of minutes admiring the sketches and

doing my best as an amateur to equate their excellence to his teaching skills. Flattery can be a potent bribe.

"I need a little more help from you. I was hoping you could point me toward a student here. Jimmy Dale Hippert."

He leaned against the wall and folded his arms. "Is this still about Beth Wilkinson?"

I nodded.

"Have you made any progress?"

"Only a little. Still haven't answered the main question—why'd she do it?"

"You think Jimmy Dale can help?"

"Don't know. I was given his name as someone who had a connection. That's all I know."

"Well, Jimmy Dale's quite a character. He's got talent, but I doubt he'll ever do much with it. He's too much a party boy."

"Does he live in a dorm?"

"He lived on campus at one time when he was in my class. That would be the address I'd have in my files. But I believe he now rents a condo north of Fruitville Road on Jefferson Street."

"You don't happen to know the address, do you?"

"Sorry, I don't. The only reason I know the general area is because Graham Parker, who's another student, told me Jimmy Dale moved near him. And I've been to Graham's place for a class party. But there are only about three condo developments there. Check with the management. He shouldn't be hard to find. It's possible he might be home this morning if he has afternoon or evening classes."

"Okay, thanks, Mr. Szostak."

"Please, it's Emile, don't forget. We're not formal here. Hope you find out what you're looking for."

"Me, too."

Jefferson was only three blocks long north of Fruitville, and Szostak was right—there were three modest one-story condominium developments, nestled into the wooded area. These were not luxury condos by any means, but a step up from dormitory living if you preferred to live alone and have your own kitchen.

It was at the second one, Northgate Commons, where the manager acknowledged a Jimmy Dale Hippert lived there. His unit was at the far end of the development, the end one closest to the parking lot in a row of eight units sided in badly stained wood with clerestory windows just below the roof ridge. A high fence surrounded a front patio, which screened the view into the condo afforded by sliding glass doors. I could tell that because the doors were slightly taller than the fence.

I reached over the top of the gate and unhooked the latch and let myself onto the tiny patio. It was ringed with pots of various sizes and shapes containing the remains of dead plants that hung limply over the sides, some trailing their dead leaves onto the concrete in a tableau of neglect. I could only suppose some former tenant left the plants, mistakenly thinking they were in good hands. If they'd been marijuana plants, they'd probably be flourishing, if I could believe Tim Olden-

burg. He probably had those in a back bedroom, carefully tended and watered. The drapes were half pulled
across the windows, allowing a glimpse of a leather
sofa, a recliner and what appeared to be a very expensive sound system. It looked like a typical bachelor pad
with books and newspapers scattered about, Nikes and
socks abandoned mid living room. I didn't see any signs
of life.

I knocked loudly on the front door. I could hear a
dog yipping a few units away, but no sound came from
within this condo. After a few minutes I knocked a second time. I was about to leave, when the door opened
and a young man in chinos and nothing else stood staring at me, not too pleasantly, I might add. He was thin
and wiry, with narrow shoulders and chest. The lack of
a shirt in this case did not mean he was showing off his
physique, but that he probably had been asleep and had
slipped on some pants to answer the door. His brown
hair was tousled and he seemed barely awake. But in
spite of the sleepiness still in his eyes, I could detect
arrogance there, as well.

"Well?" he asked irritably. I gave him the benefit
of the doubt and attributed his attitude to having been
awakened by my knock.

"Are you Jimmy Dale Hippert?"

He looked me up and down. "Who are you?"

"Emma Daniels."

He yawned and leaned against the door frame. "So?"

"I was a friend of Beth Wilkinson's."

"And?"

Boy, he was a real talker, this one. I could see I was going to have to drag any information out of him bit by bit, if he deigned to tell me anything at all. And he obviously had no intention of inviting me in. Not that I would go.

I decided to act as cool as he was, so I said very casually, "I was talking to Timothy Oldenburg yesterday—" he raised his eyebrows at this "—and he told me he borrowed money from you to pay for an abortion for Beth Wilkinson. I just wanted to check it out."

This made him stand up straight and cram his hands into his hip pockets, which caused his scrawny elbows to jut out. He looked like a stork standing at attention. His face took on the expression of a televangelist facing up to the devil. "Tim's a damn liar. I never did no such thing."

"It's not like it's illegal. There's nothing wrong with paying for one. It certainly wouldn't get you into trouble."

"Hell, I know that, though there's a lot of frickin' screwballs down here who go around blowin' up clinics and killing doctors. And that's beside the point. I never paid for no abortion."

"Did you know Beth?"

"I knew who she was. Never had anything to do with her."

"I thought you were Tim's roommate."

"I was for a while. But he thought he and Beth were too frickin' good for the likes of me. He never brought her around."

"Did you know she had an abortion?"

"Hell, no. Tim didn't exactly share his sex life with me. In fact, he pretty much ignored me. As far as I was concerned, that was fine 'cause I thought he was an ass."

"Well, okay, then. If that's all you've got to say, I'll go now. Thanks for talking to me." I hoped he caught my sarcasm.

Jimmy Dale said nothing but turned and walked back into the living room, shut the door resoundingly and pulled the drapes shut.

EIGHTEEN

I REALLY DIDN'T KNOW what to make of the kid other than the fact he was obnoxious. I called Cal on my cell phone once I was back in my car, and he answered on the third ring.

"Hi, it's me. Just wanted you to know I talked to Jimmy Dale." I told him about getting directions from Szostak and my conversation with Tim's former roommate.

"He sounds like a real winner," Cal said. "But can we discount what he said simply because he's so disagreeable?"

"That's what I'm struggling with. I want to believe Tim because he seemed like such a nice kid and not believe Jimmy Dale because he's the opposite. But like you said, nothing Beth told me was the truth, so why should I believe Tim? Jimmy Dale, as churlish as he is, might be the only one who's giving me the straight scoop."

"Too bad we can't give them all lie detector tests." Cal sounded as discouraged as I felt. "So what are you going to do now?"

"I don't know. Go home, I guess. I've got to pay a little more attention to Mark. He won't be here much longer. I've barely given him the time of day since he got here, and I'm always wishing he would visit me more often. Not a good way to encourage him to come back."

"Well, we both can mull it over. Maybe our subconscious will pop up with an answer."

"You've got more faith than I do. I wonder if we haven't reached a dead end here. Frankly, I don't know where else to go with it."

"Don't beat yourself up. How many people would have pursued it as far as you have? One of your strongest traits is persistence. I might add, for better or for worse."

"I don't think that was quite a compliment."

"Ninety percent compliment, ten percent dismay."

"Try to concentrate on the ninety percent, will you?"

As I drove home to fix Mark some lunch, I realized he was perfectly capable of doing it himself. But as I told Cal, I needed to spend more time with him. The week was going by too fast.

When we finished eating, he decided to go for a run on the beach. "I've probably gained ten pounds feeding my face and lolling about. I don't want to turn into a total lump," he said. "I need to get some exercise." Mark normally went to the gym and worked out regularly. A few days off wasn't going to kill him, but I was glad he was going out because I'd decided I should call Caronis and advise him of the two incidents the day before. I was hoping he'd convince me they were freak accidents and I shouldn't worry about it, and a little afraid he would think I was overreacting. On the other hand, if there was something to them, I didn't want him bawling me out later because I'd neglected my duty to tell him.

"Mrs. Daniels," he greeted me pleasantly when I reached him. "What's up?"

"A couple of things happened yesterday that I'm a little concerned about."

"Tell me about them," he said.

So I told him in detail about the accident and what the manager at the auto shop had told me about the tie rods. I also described my close call in the restaurant parking lot.

"Okay," he said. "I understand you're concerned because the two incidents happened so close together. If you think they were deliberate, do you have any idea why someone would do that?"

Here was the sticky part. I wasn't going to tell Detective Caronis about what I'd been doing to uncover the motive behind Beth's scam. In the first place, he'd probably dismiss me as a hysterical old woman. And in the second place, he'd think I was interfering in police business. I'd decided in advance what I was going to say.

"I just thought maybe it was connected to the scam in some way."

"Not likely, Mrs. Daniels. One perp is dead and the other in jail."

"I guess you're right."

"However, if anything else happens that makes you suspicious, I want you to call me. Okay?"

"Sure, I'll do that."

Well, so much for that. My worst fears were realized. He thought I was a ditz, and he had not convinced me that my instincts were wrong.

AFTER MARK CAME BACK from his run, he showered, put on fresh chinos and a T-shirt and went out on the balcony with a book.

I went to my bedroom to put away some clothes I'd taken out of the dryer.

When I got back to the living room, Mark was standing in the middle of it, staring out the window at the Gulf. "Is something wrong?" I asked. Something about his posture made me ask.

He turned to me and sighed. "My boss just called. They've got some kind of crisis going on in the office. He called to ask if you were well enough that I might be able to go back and help them out."

"And you said?"

"I said yes, Ma. I've been feeling pretty guilty about lying to them that you were sick. And there's nothing I can do about Cindy at this point. It's up to her now."

"Do you have to leave right this minute?"

"Yeah, I do. But what are you going to do about transportation? Once I'm gone you'll be carless."

"That's okay. I don't need one today. I'll ask Cal to take me to a rental agency in the morning."

"You're sure?"

"I'm sure. And I should get mine back in a couple of days. Hate to see you go, but I'm so glad you could come, even if you had to tell a fib. And I don't think your nose has grown so anyone will notice."

"What?" Mark obviously didn't get my joke.

"Pinocchio, honey. I read it to you when you were a child."

He didn't even comment, just made a face and went to pack.

SHORTLY AFTER MARK LEFT, Jean Jacobs came to the door.

"You're out almost as much as I am anymore," she said, trying to look upset with me without much success. Jean might get cross on the subject of her daughter-in-law, but otherwise she was normally a sunny person. There was little else that could put her in a bad mood.

"Oh, Jean, I tried to call you back, but you weren't home. Come on in." Actually, by now I'd forgotten about her call. Or maybe I'd been subconsciously avoiding it.

She sat in one of the side chairs while I sat on the sofa, straightening up the throw pillows that Mark had strewn about.

"What's up?" I asked

"Oh, I'm so pissed off at Barb I wanted to bitch about her to someone."

Here we go again, I thought.

"Poor you, you got elected!" she continued, grinning sheepishly. "Ross is tired of listening to me, and you're the only one outside of the family who knows about it."

I had more than enough on my mind right now, but I couldn't be rude to her. So I put on my eager-to-hear face and prayed she wouldn't stay long.

She proceeded to tell me every hurtful thing that her daughter-in-law had ever done to her or Ross or Sam. It left me wondering why Sam had put up with her for so long. My attention straying, I began watching a pelican soar back and forth across my window on the updrafts caused by the building, when she said something that made me sit bolt upright.

"Would you say that again, please?" I wasn't sure I heard right.

"I said that the whole Hippert family can go jump in the Gulf as far as I'm concerned."

"Barb's maiden name is Hippert?"

"Yes. Why?"

"She wouldn't by any chance have a brother by the name of Jimmy Dale, would she?"

Jean thought for a moment. "Jimmy Dale. I think that's a cousin of hers. Never met him, though. Do you know him?"

"Oh, I met him recently."

"What's he like? The rest of the clan doesn't impress me much."

"I only talked to him for a couple of minutes. I'd say he probably fit in well with the family."

Jean smirked. "A typical Hippert, huh?"

I wanted to change the subject before she asked me how I came to meet him. "Is Sam dealing with it any better?"

"Not well at all. I wonder if there's a support group for husbands who get dumped."

"I'm sure there is—they have a group for everything." Mark could have used one, too, I thought.

Just then the telephone rang, and I excused myself to answer it in the kitchen.

"Is this Emma Daniels?"

"Yes." I didn't recognize the voice.

"This is Officer Spaulding from the Sarasota Police Department. Your son, Mark, has been in a car accident and is in the emergency room at Memorial Hospital."

Suddenly my vision dimmed and I thought I was going to faint. I sat down in one of the dinette chairs before I fell. "Is he hurt bad?"

"I don't believe it's life threatening, ma'am. He's got some broken bones and maybe internal injuries."

"I'll be right there." I hung up and sat there a few seconds until I was sure I could make it out of the kitchen.

The minute I walked back into the living room, Jean looked at me in alarm and said, "Emma, what is it?"

"It's Mark. He's been hurt in an accident. Could you take me to the hospital? My car's in the garage." I didn't intend to bring her up to date on that score. I just wanted to get to the hospital and fast. My throat was constricted with anxiety.

She came over and hugged me tightly. "I know he's going to be all right, Emma. Now, where's your purse?" She got my purse, took my arm and led me out the door over to her place, where she picked up her pocketbook and keys, and then down the elevator and out to the parking lot. I was in such shock, I let her lead me like a child.

She guided me carefully into the passenger seat of her Cadillac, got in the driver's seat and nearly flew out of the lot. I was afraid we, too, would be accident victims as she exceeded the speed limit by a wide margin going up the island, across the north bridge to Osprey Avenue and north to the hospital. My heart was pounding wildly by now, a mixture of apprehension over Mark's condition and fear for my life as we narrowly missed collisions twice when Jean gunned it through two yellow-on-the-verge-of-red lights. She pulled up to the emergency room door and let me out, saying she'd be in as soon as she parked the car.

A tall, slender policeman was standing by the admissions desk.

"Officer Spaulding?" I asked. I assumed he was the one who'd called me.

"Mrs. Daniels?"

"Yes. Where's my son?"

"They're examining him now. They should be out to talk to you soon." I could tell he'd dealt often with anxious relatives of accident victims. His voice was reassuring, his demeanor kind.

"Can you tell me what happened?"

"He went through a stoplight at Beneva and Bee Ridge. He swerved to miss a car going west on Bee Ridge and hit a telephone pole. The car was totaled. He's lucky to be alive."

"No one else was hurt?"

"No. He barely missed the other car."

"Can I see him now?"

"Not till the doctors are through. Just have a seat in the waiting room."

I joined the half dozen other people waiting there and realized it was just days ago I'd passed by here on the way to the morgue to identify Beth. I could easily have been going there to identify my son. Mark was such a good driver I could hardly believe he'd gone through a red light, but he probably never saw it. Although he hadn't said so, I suspected that the crisis at work had him worried, and Cindy's troubles were always at the back of his mind. Maybe I should have discouraged him from leaving immediately and suggested he wait till morning. But it never occurred to me it wasn't safe for him to be on the road. My poor, poor baby.

Jean came hurrying in and sat down beside me, and I gave her what little information I'd gleaned from Officer Spaulding. She took my hand and held it tightly. "Mark's healthy and strong. He'll heal quickly."

I wanted to say it helps to have a positive outlook on life, and Mark had a way to go on that. But I still felt I would betray his trust if I told Jean all his troubles now.

It was almost an hour before anyone called my name. Finally a white-jacketed man stood in the doorway and asked for Mrs. Daniels. He took me to a quiet corner of the room and sat down beside me.

"We're going to admit your son for at least a day or two. He has a couple of broken ribs, a laceration on his left leg, a broken left arm and various bruises and contusions. Luckily the break was a simple one, no surgery is needed. He's going to be very sore for a while, but he'll be just fine."

Relief flooded through me. It was serious, but far from life threatening. "Can I see him now?"

"Sure. We'll take him upstairs shortly, but you can talk to him for a minute. Let me take you to his cubicle."

I followed him back to the treatment area, a series of spaces divided by heavy duck curtains. Mark was in the third one on the left. His eyes were closed, his arm at his side was encased in a cast from his wrist to his elbow, and showing above the blanket that covered him was a portion of the tape that bound his broken ribs.

I leaned over and said "Mark?" softly in his ear.

He opened his eyes. "Hi, Mom. Sorry about this."

"Honestly, Mark. I'm going to have to take your driving privileges away and cut off your television for a month." I was parroting something I'd said to him about fifteen years earlier when he'd put a dent in the family car.

His eyes widened, and then he started to roar, but caught himself. "Please don't make me laugh. It hurts my ribs. It's déjà vu all over again!"

"I'm so damn glad you're alive and not hurt any worse. Cars can be replaced, although when you were a teen all I could think of was the repair bill. Moms of teens tend to get focused on all the small stuff instead of the big picture."

"That's a relief. I was afraid this time you'd take away my allowance and not let me have any dessert for a month." Tit for tat. His sense of humor seemed intact.

We worked very hard to keep the conversation in that vein until they came to take him upstairs.

"Jean Jacobs brought me over," I told him. "She's out in the waiting room. I'll bring her upstairs to see you if that's okay. We won't stay but a minute."

"You haven't told her about Cindy, have you?"

"No, that's your business."

"I just couldn't stand to have her making over me out of pity."

"Don't worry. She's all wrapped up in her own son's troubles."

"Thanks, Mom."

I went back and got Jean, and we went to the third floor to Mark's room. They had just transferred him into the bed when we got there. We chatted a few minutes before I told Jean I thought we ought to leave, that Mark needed rest. He gave me a look of gratitude as I swept her out of the room.

Jean then dropped me off at the airport to pick up a rental car. All the way home I fought to keep my mind on my driving and off the string of disasters that had plagued us. I could see how easily Mark could have been distracted. The last thing we needed was another accident. I carefully stayed within the speed limit, which caused the cars behind me great distress, and they'd whip around me at the first opportunity, giving me the evil eye, if not the finger. What a lot of pent-up anger there is out there.

NINETEEN

WHEN I GOT HOME, I DEBATED briefly whether Cindy should be informed of Mark's accident, before realizing I didn't know how to reach her. What about the people at work? He was able to call them, and I was sure he would want to be the one to do it.

I frittered away what little was left of the afternoon, made myself a light supper and drove back to the hospital again.

Mark looked better than he had in the afternoon. He said he'd talked to his boss, who was very sympathetic and told him to take his time about returning to work.

"I hope he doesn't decide I'm a screw off."

"What about their crisis? Can they handle it without you?" I asked.

"Actually, when I talked to him, things had calmed down a bit. As it turned out, I probably didn't need to go at all. The guy gets easily spooked. Tends to make snap decisions without thinking things through. He's always been an alarmist." He shrugged.

That made me utterly furious, but no use in upsetting Mark by venting to him.

So I said, "I'm sure he realizes you've had some bad

luck. The important thing is for you to concentrate on getting well. Try to forget the unpleasant stuff."

"Right, Mom." That was a rote answer if I ever heard one.

THE NEXT MORNING I WAS getting ready to visit Mark when he called me.

"I'm being discharged at eleven," he said. "Bring me some clothes, will you? The ones I was wearing are a mess."

I wondered what had happened to the clothes he'd had with him. Probably in the trunk of the car at the scrap yard. I'd have to go there and retrieve whatever valuables were in it when I had a chance.

"That's great news. I'll be there."

A quick trip to the nearest Walmart was sufficient to buy a set of underwear, shorts and a tee, which I put into a tote bag I'd brought from home. Mark was sitting in a chair when I arrived, wearing one of those awful hospital gowns with a sheet thrown over his exposed legs. He was impatiently drumming his fingers on the arm of the chair.

"Would you mind leaving the room?" he asked. "When I get up, there's not much left to the imagination."

"Like I've never seen your butt before?"

He glowered at me and I hastily made an exit.

When he called me back into the room, I was shocked to see a large bandage just below his left knee. His legs had been covered by sheets or blankets up until now.

"How many stitches did you have?"

"Twenty-one, I think."

"I guess you're going to have to forgo the Mr. America contest."

"The worst part was they had to shave my leg. How do you women stand doing that?"

"You have no idea what martyrs we are to fashion dictates."

"Makes me glad to be a guy."

Much to his disgust, the nurses insisted he ride in a wheelchair to the exit. I went to get the car while an orderly pushed him to the hospital door.

I noticed how he winced as he lowered himself gingerly into the passenger seat of the Aveo. "As long as you were renting, why didn't you get some big old thing I could get into easily?" he asked in a petulant voice.

"Because this is what my insurance company is willing to pay for. And for once you're going to have to let me drive you," I said. "That may be the worst punishment of all." I said it jokingly, but there was more than a bit of truth in it. He's always felt more comfortable when at the wheel of the car. Maybe it was a male thing.

"I'm sure you drive just fine," he said to placate me. "But you know what a hang-up I have about needing to be the driver."

"Even after yesterday?" I knew that was an awful thing to say. I'd promised myself I wouldn't bring up his culpability. But it slipped out without thinking.

"That's what I want to talk to you about. I wasn't

going to mention it, but when the police came today, I changed my mind."

I was on my way out of the parking lot, but when he said that, I pulled into a parking space and stopped. "What on earth are you talking about?"

"The reason I went through the red light was my brakes didn't work. Yesterday I thought that my car had some kind of manufacturing flaw. You know it only has twenty-five thousand miles on it, and the brakes shouldn't go bad that soon."

"My God, Mark, you should have told me."

"This morning a cop came to see me," he went on, "and said it looked like the brake line had been cut. The brake fluid had leaked out and that's why they failed."

"Couldn't that have happened accidentally?"

"They didn't think so. It was too clean a cut."

If I'd been frightened at the Galleon the other night, now I was numb with dread. Why would someone do that? Why would they want to hurt Mark? And then, of course, it dawned on me: someone had deliberately tampered with Mark's car thinking I'd drive it while mine was in the garage. It had to be the same person who'd tried to run me down in the restaurant parking lot. And, I now realized, really did tamper with my Civic. His car had been in a spot clearly marked as my visitor's parking space. It couldn't be a coincidence. It had taken a while, but I was getting the message loud and clear.

When I got back to La Hacienda, I was going to leave my rental at the opposite end of the parking lot so no one could identify it as one I was driving.

I could tell Mark was staring at me. "What's going on, Mom? You've been acting a little strange ever since I got here. I don't think this was a random act." Unfortunately, Mark knew about my last "adventure" some months before when I had a couple of narrow escapes.

I turned to him, trying my best to look guileless, and said with a shrug, "Mark, I don't know what to tell you." That was true. I didn't say I didn't know, just that there was nothing I could tell him now. I had grave suspicions, of course, but I was keeping them to myself for now.

He said nothing, but turned and looked out the side window as if fascinated with the traffic on the nearby street. I'm sure he was trying to get himself under control so he wouldn't say what he was thinking.

When I felt sufficiently calm again, I pulled out of the parking lot and drove toward Siesta Key. Neither of us said anything for a while. Mark, I imagine, was having dark thoughts about how I was stonewalling him. And I was wondering how much longer I could continue to do so. I'd crossed the bridge and was on Higel Avenue on the north end of the island, when Mark spoke again.

"Does this have something to do with the girl who drowned?"

"I can't imagine why it would." Now the lies flowed easily from me, but I kept kidding myself there was at least a slim possibility it had nothing to do with Beth. Perhaps the cops were wrong about the brake line being cut. Maybe my tie rods were just old and poorly maintained. Though in my heart I knew that was very unlikely. "It might have been someone's twisted idea of a joke or they got the wrong car. I've heard rumors that some retired Mafia live in the area. Maybe they live at La Hacienda, and someone mistook your car for theirs." Did I really think he'd swallow such nonsense?

"You gotta be kidding me," he said sarcastically.

"Just trying to come up with a plausible scenario."

He shook his head in disgust and was silent the rest of the way home.

A message on my answering machine told me to please call Detective Salkowitz at the police department. I knew it must be about the brake tampering. I returned the call, but was told he was out on a case and he'd call me later in the afternoon.

I fixed salad and egg salad sandwiches for lunch, and then Mark said he'd like to lie down for a while. He moved like an old man, gingerly testing every gesture or step to determine the limits of his sore, bruised muscles. The limits were very circumscribed at this point.

He went into the bedroom and closed the door, and I went to the kitchen and called Cal. He said he was doing his laundry. I told him about Mark's accident and what the police had told him.

"Jesus Christ!" he exclaimed. "He could have been killed. Or you, too, for that matter. This kind of puts a new light on things, doesn't it?"

"Yeah, it does. And now Mark's getting very curious about what's going on. I don't know what to do, Cal. If I tell him all, he will totally freak out. He needs to concentrate on getting better, not worry about his old mom."

"Why don't you lay it on the police. Let them handle it."

"I know I should. I told Caronis about the tie rods in my car, and he kind of blew me off. But he probably doesn't know about Mark's brake line. I doubt anyone over there has put two and two together."

"That would be the safest thing to do."

"Yeah, I was the one who kept urging Beth to go to the police. Maybe they'll take more interest in Beth's case now."

"That's all the more reason to let them deal with it."

I hung up and went out on the balcony and tried to read a book I'd been dipping into for over two weeks. As usual, my mind wouldn't concentrate on it. Around two, the phone rang. I thought it was probably Detective Salkowitz.

"Hi, it's Jean. Just wanted to know how Mark's doing."

"I brought him home this morning."

"Oh, I'm so glad. I'll bet he's sore."

"God, yes. He can barely move. I think the ribs are the worst."

We talked a few minutes about their upcoming sailing trip to Key West before she changed the subject.

"Say," she said, "did you hear about Blanche Kelly down on four?"

"No. I think I'm out of the loop. I never know what goes on around here."

"You ought to go to our Tuesday ladies' meetings."

"Spare me." The women sit around crocheting things for the Christmas Bazaar and arguing over how to spend the money they earn. Usually they buy hideous statuary or fountains for the grounds which I keep hoping will be destroyed by lightning or some other act of God. I've even been tempted to "accidentally" run over some of it.

"Blanche lost her husband about the time Paul died," Jean said. "He had lung cancer. It was awful. Anyway, I heard she just got bilked out of thousands of dollars. Poor thing."

It was like an electric shock went through me. Surely Beth hadn't been involved in another scam. There must be an epidemic of this going around, I thought. "How'd they do it?"

"It was some kind of Ponzi scheme, I think. I don't really understand it, but she invested in a group that was supposed to be buying fine European antique furniture for resale, and they'd pay her big interest on her money. The thing is they paid off subscribers with money from other subscribers until the whole thing fell apart and the last ones in lost a mint."

"That's terrible."

"I heard she lost most of the money she got from life insurance."

"She must be sick about it."

"She is. In fact, she's so upset she's thinking of moving back north to be near her kids. She says there's nothing but a bunch of crooks running around Florida cheating everyone out of their money."

"I doubt that it's any worse here than anywhere else. But I do think they tend to pick on older people. And let's face it, there are plenty of older people here."

"That's because they usually have the money available. And maybe they're easier to bilk."

"I expect that's true," said one who was bilked.

I went back out on the balcony after we hung up and thought about Blanche Kelly instead of reading my book. Was it a mere coincidence that both of us had been victims of a scam? Wasn't it strange that both our husbands had died about the same time and we each lost part of our insurance settlements? Could it possibly be that somebody, singular or plural, was able to find out when widows received large settlements and targeted them for their schemes? The more I thought about it, the more intriguing it seemed, and I got so caught up in the possibilities I knew I had to check it out.

I didn't know Blanche Kelly from Santa Claus, but I looked up her number and called her. She had a high, timid voice and sounded as though she was at least in her eighties.

"This is Emma Daniels, Blanche," I said. "I live on the eleventh floor here at La Hacienda. I just heard via the grapevine about your unfortunate experience with some investments. I don't mean to be nosy, but I really need to talk to you about it. Would you mind if I come down and see you?"

"Please do," she said. "I don't mind talking about it. I'd like the whole world to know what scum these people are." That was good. She sounded ready to pour out her soul.

Blanche looked just as she sounded: old, frail, tiny in stature, but full of gumption. She was mad, and she made no bones about it. Her thin white hair had been teased into a halo, and her eyes were full of righteous indignation. She wore a flower-print dress that hung from her frame. I wondered if she'd lost weight since the scam was discovered.

She invited me to sit down on her sofa, rattan with cushions covered in pink and green stripes. "Can I get you something to drink, dear?" In spite of it all, her manners were still intact.

I told her I'd just had lunch, so she settled into a Boston rocker. With a pile of books on the floor on one side of it and newspapers on the other, I assumed this was where Blanche spent most of her time.

"So what would you like to know?" she asked.

"I've been hearing about these scams recently, and it's frightening. It could happen to any of us. I know it must have been terrible to find out what these people were doing to you."

"Oh, yes. Isn't it awful? I'm so glad Ralph's not around to know about it. The people who got me involved gave false names and addresses, so the police haven't been able to arrest anyone. I lost most of our life's savings, and I might have to move in with my kids." She was on the verge of tears, and my heart went out to her. At least they stole only a portion of my money, not enough to greatly affect my lifestyle, at least not at this time. But who knew how long I might live? I could run out of resources before I ran out of breaths.

"I'm so very sorry, Blanche. That was a terrible thing they did. I hope the cops can catch them eventually."

"Me, too," she said, "though even then I might not get my money back." The tears had begun to slip out of her eyes.

I had a Kleenex in my pocket which I gave to her. I wished I had another for myself. I was deeply touched by her plight.

But I needed to ask the question I had come for. "I don't mean to be prying, but I wondered if you could tell me what insurance company your husband had a policy with."

"Yeoman Life. Why do you ask?"

Yeoman Life. That was Paul's life insurance company, too. Maybe it was a coincidence, but I didn't have a good feeling about it.

"I have a hunch about something. If it turns out to be true, I'll explain it to you later. Okay?"

"Well, it sounds very mysterious. But if you can help me at all, I'd be very appreciative."

It might be too late to help her, as well as too late for me. But if I could prevent any future tragedies, I had to follow up on my suspicions.

TWENTY

I WAS FEELING TOO ANTSY to sit around the house. My mind was going in a million directions, though nothing was becoming any clearer. I decided to go to the Yeoman Life office and talk to the manager. Find out who besides the employees knew about these insurance payments. It seems very hard to keep anything confidential anymore. Thanks to computers, it's as though the whole world's aware of everything you do. And that is where the swindlers come in.

Mark was sound asleep, so I left him a note saying I needed to run some errands. I put my folding umbrella into my shoulder bag just in case. They were forecasting heavy rain but said it probably wouldn't get to Sarasota till evening. But who can trust weather forecasters?

The Yeoman Life office is near the airport on 41, and I was there in twenty-five minutes. It's a one-story flat-roofed brick building with a small, neat lawn and a parking lot in the rear.

I'd never been to the office before because Paul had always handled the insurance, and when he died, a solicitous agent came to my home to bring me the check. What he really wanted was for me to invest the money in one of their annuities. I managed to resist his glowing endorsement however.

Inside the front door was a counter for customer service and a perky young girl eager to wait on me.

"May I speak to the manager please?" I asked her.

"Let me check and see if she's busy with anyone," she said, ducking around the corner. She came back almost immediately and, pointing to the corridor that ran from the front to the rear of the building along the left outside wall, said, "First door down the hall."

I thanked her and walked toward the office.

The door was open and a woman was standing with her back to me putting a manual on a bookshelf. When she turned around, I was startled to see that it was Barb Jacobs. I remembered, then, her remark at the dinner party that she lived near the insurance office where she worked. I never dreamed it was Yeoman Life.

She seemed equally surprised to see me. But after a half second, she quickly gathered herself together and turned on the charm. "Mrs. Daniels. What a surprise. How nice to see you." I wondered if she suspected her mother-in-law was bad-mouthing her and decided to win me over with her graciousness. "Have a seat." She waved to the chair across the desk from hers. "Can I get you a cup of coffee?"

I declined the coffee and sat in the chair, trying to take in the room without being obvious about it. It was small by most standards for the person-in-charge and windowless. The overhead fluorescent light was flickering annoyingly like a tic, and the furniture was generic and plain, although it was dusted and polished to a high sheen. Where the reception area had been freshly painted and papered and had attractive floral prints on the wall, the walls here were insipid beige, and I got the distinct impression that the company held tight reins on the budget for nonpublic areas. The room, however, was extremely neat, compulsively so. The items on her desk—in- and out-box, pen holder, stapler, telephone, paper-clip holder—were lined up in a perfect row across the front edge of the desk. There was a spotless desk blotter and letter opener and one envelope, face down, that she'd been in the process of opening. No other papers were in sight. Even the wastebasket was empty. The rest of the room was equally immaculate: two four-drawer files, their tops without the usual clutter; a bookcase holding volumes of insurance regulations arranged according to size; a copying machine; a stand with a fax machine; and in the corner, a computer with a cover over it. The only thing on the wall was a freebie calendar. It looked like nobody worked there. It made me wonder what she did.

"You're the manager here?" I asked.

"Yes, I've worked here for seven years, have been manager for three. I'm surprised you didn't know that since I'm sure Jean must talk about me." She said this with a caustic edge, giving me a forced little smile. She even gave a slight toss to her dark hair, which was cut in a pageboy style too severe for her model-pretty face. Though she was being the epitome of frosty politeness, I could understand how she irritated the hell out of Jean.

I wasn't going to let her get to me the way she got to her mother-in-law. "She's mentioned you now and then in passing. But she's never talked about your work."

She rewarded me with a look of pure disdain. I'm sure I hit a nerve. She then yawned, a fake yawn, which she covered with her hand, and said, "Excuse me," which translated meant "you are boring me." She then sat up a little straighter, if possible, and said, "And what can I do for you today?"

"I was wondering if someone outside of your company could get access to your files."

Her expression turned dark. She picked up the letter opener by the sharp end and began bouncing the handle of it on her desk as if she were tapping out an SOS on jungle drums. I don't think she even realized she was doing it.

"Of course not. All our files are confidential."

"They're in a computer, right?"

"Of course."

"Couldn't an outsider get into your computer files?"

"We have a series of passwords that one must enter to access them. Why do you ask?"

"I wondered if anyone outside of Yeoman Life could have known I received a large insurance payment in the past year. I seem to be getting a lot of unsolicited calls wanting me to invest my money in this or that fund. I was curious as to why that was happening." Actually, I'd only a few calls of this kind right after Paul died, but it was the only way I could think of to explain my presence here.

She stopped bouncing the letter opener and now held it in front of her like a shield, clasping each end with a thumb and forefinger. "I think that's easy to explain. As soon as an obituary is published in the paper, it triggers those kinds of calls. And when estates go to probate, the results are public record."

"So you don't think it's at all alarming that people are coming out of the woodwork trying to get their hands on my money. And it has nothing to do with my insurance settlement."

"Absolutely not. We pride ourselves on our discretion." She tossed the letter opener onto the desktop. "Now if you don't mind, I'm very busy today."

Busy doing what? I could see no signs of activity in her office. She probably had to go crack the whip over her underlings who were grinding away in a dismal back room.

I stood up to go. I picked up my purse off the floor and said, "By the way, I understand you're kin to Jimmy Dale Hippert."

Her thin lips became even thinner, almost disappearing as she struggled not to react. "He's a distant cousin," she said in a tone of voice that relegated him to the ranks of the unwashed. "Our paths do not cross." She almost literally turned up her nose at the mere thought of it. She didn't ask how I knew him.

"I appreciate your help," I said, though she hadn't been the least enlightening, and left her to her bean counting or whatever it was she did. The young girl at the front counter gave me a cheerful "Have a good day" as I left.

I sat in my rental car in the parking lot reviewing what she'd told me. If Yeoman Life had such a stringent security system that no outsiders could get into files, that didn't rule out employees from using information for their own gain. Presumably they all had access. Was one of the employees involved in devising scams to strip widows of their death benefits? Or were they feeding the information to someone else for a kickback? It seemed too coincidental for two of us at La Hacienda to be ripped off after our insurance checks came.

I was considering all this when the back door opened and Barb Jacobs came out and got into a Volvo station wagon that was parked beside the door. I was at the far corner of the lot, and she never noticed me. Why would she be leaving the office at two forty-five in the afternoon? I was curious as hell, and on the spur of the moment decided to follow her. I argued with myself as I waited until she'd gone around the building and down the driveway. Who did I think I was: Spencer? Wasn't it kind of silly for me to go sneaking around following people? But damn, it was too serendipitous an opportunity to pass up. I waited until she turned south on 41 before I drove down the driveway. I let a couple of cars go by, then pulled out onto the street, keeping her far enough ahead that she wouldn't notice me. She drove down to Ringling Boulevard, through downtown to Fruitville Road. I'll be darned, I thought. She's going to see Jimmy Dale.

And that's exactly what she did. She turned left onto Jefferson and pulled into Northgate Commons. At this point I didn't know what to do. Their meeting right after my visit to Barb spelled collusion to me. There were too many links for this to be a coincidence.

But I still had no concrete evidence for the police. I needed more than conjecture. I decided to park near the front entrance to the development and walk along the edge of the parking lot to the row of condos where Jimmy Dale lived. Remembering the fence that surrounded his front patio, I wondered if I could successfully hunker down behind it and try to overhear their conversation. If the sliding doors were closed, I'd be out of luck. But it was one of those gorgeous days that invites one to open all the windows, and I prayed that Jimmy Dale had done just that. I didn't encounter anyone in the parking lot. With any luck, no one would see me hanging around outside his fence. From the time I visited before, I had the impression that younger working-class people lived here, so I prayed most everyone was gone. If someone did stroll by, I'd pretend I was pulling weeds, which obviously needed to be done.

As soon as I was outside his condo, I could hear voices distinctly, even though they were speaking in low tones. There was little, if any, traffic noise here, and their voices carried clearly across the small patio. It was definitely Barb and Jimmy Dale who were talking.

"You stupid little twerp." I could hear the anger in Barb's voice. "Have you been talking to Emma Daniels?"

"Aw, the bitch came poundin' on my door askin' me

if I loaned Tim money for Beth's abortion. I told her I didn't know nothin' about any abortion."

"And that's all you said?"

"I swear it."

"Then why was she over at Yeoman Life just now asking if anybody outside of the company could get at her records?"

"That don't follow. What's one got to do with the other?"

"Idiot!" She sounded furious. "I think she's beginning to piece things together."

"Well, shee-it. She shouldn't be around long to bug us. I fixed her brakes. When the loose tie rods didn't kill her but only smashed up her old junker, I saw the car in her visitor's space and figured she was using that. So I cut the brake lines. She'll smash herself up good, and the cops will write it off as an accident. They'd never figure the connection."

Even though I knew about the tie rods and the brakes, his confirmation made me almost ill. It was the casual way he said it that made it so utterly chilling.

"Like everything else you do, you probably screwed it up. She's still alive and kicking. Or was fifteen minutes ago. You probably cut the wrong line."

"I made small cuts on purpose so it would take a while for the brake fluid to leak out. I didn't want it to happen right after she visited me."

"Christ, it'll probably be next week before it works. This woman is getting too damn nosy. The police seem to have written it off as strictly Beth's little project. I don't want anything to make them change their minds."

"So what are you going to do?"

"I need to use your phone. Where is it?"

"Back in the bedroom I use as an office. I'll show you."

Damn, now I was going to miss the telephone conversation. It was my bad luck he didn't have a phone in the living room. I hoped they'd come back where I could hear them after her call. Since I'd been squatting so my head wouldn't show above the fence, my back and knees were beginning to feel as though I'd never straighten up again. I finally knelt on the grass to give my back a break, even though I knew my white slacks would acquire green grass stains on the knees that would no doubt defy the strongest bleach.

It seemed like a very long while that they were gone, though my uncomfortable position probably was skewing my perception of time. Fortunately, no one had walked by to see me cowering behind the patio fence. I was glad his condo was far back from the road and obscured by other rows of condominiums so that no one driving by on Jefferson could see me. I only had to be alert as to when Barb was leaving so I could make a hasty retreat. There was a large hedge of oleander a few feet away that defined the back of the property, and I decided I could quickly hide behind it. That would probably be safer than trying to get to my car.

As the moments ticked away, I became more and more concerned. They were probably finishing their conversation in the bedroom, and I was afraid I wouldn't have adequate warning when Barb left. I was trying to decide if I should head for the oleander hedge immediately, when someone grabbed my left arm and twisted it painfully behind my back, almost forcing me flat on my face. I put out my right hand and caught myself just before my nose would have slammed into the ground. Then the gate in the fence swung open, and I heard Barb's voice. "Good work, Jimmy Dale." I couldn't raise my head high enough to see her. "Bring her inside." I couldn't believe this was happening to me. My heart began pounding wildly in fear.

He jerked my arm upward, pulling me without resistance to my feet. I was in such pain I had no choice. I was certain he was going to break it. He pushed me in front of him across the patio and into his living room. Barb followed and quickly shut the front door and sliding glass doors and pulled the drapes.

She dragged a dinette chair from the small eating area and placed it in the middle of the living room. I now noticed she held a carving knife at her side. "Sit her down there," she commanded. He pushed me over to it, released my arm and, putting his hands on my shoulders, slammed me down into the seat. Not only did that reverberate up my spine, but my arm was numb and tingling from being twisted. I rubbed it up and down its length, trying to restore my circulation. What were they going to do to me? After learning it was Jimmy Dale who cut the brake lines, I knew they were utterly ruthless.

"Have you got any rope or anything we can tie her up with?" Barb asked as she looked at me as though I were one of the hideous blobs of jellyfish that wash up on the beach from time to time. She shook her head at me. "You're one dumb broad. If you're going to play detective, you'd better take some lessons first."

"How did you know I was outside?" I kept my voice as even as possible. My stomach was churning so, I was afraid I'd lose my lunch, but I didn't want them to know how terrified I was. My fear would only serve to their advantage.

"Jimmy Dale needed something from his car, and he went out the back door to get it. And there you were, kneeling in front of the fence with your back to him. I mean, how stupid can you get?"

I didn't have an answer. I knew I was, indeed, stupid.

Jimmy Dale had gone into the back of the condo and had returned with a long extension cord. "This is the best I can do."

"Tie her hands behind her, then. Have you got another for her feet?"

"I can probably find one." He roughly pulled my hands back and wrapped the cord tightly around my wrists. I thought he was going to cut off the circulation altogether, but he stopped just short. I wondered if he did this kind of thing as a matter of course. He seemed pretty adept at it.

He went into a bedroom again and came back with another cord. "I had to take this off my bed lamp. I'm not going to have any light in there tonight."

"Don't be such a whiner. You worry about the damnedest things," Barb said in her most dismissive voice.

He tied my ankles together as tightly as my wrists. Then he stood up. "Okay. Now what?"

"My son knows I went to the Yeoman Life office," I said, willing my voice not to tremble. "If I don't come home soon, he's going to have the police checking it out." God, how I wished that were true.

"I'll just tell them you saw me and left, and I had no idea where you went."

"But someone in your office must have known you left right after I did. They can put two and two together."

A flicker of worry passed over Barb's features. "I told them I had a doctor's appointment."

"You think they can't check that out?" I tried to act astonished. I didn't know how much good this was doing, but I was desperate to try anything to postpone the inevitable. She hadn't counted on having to account for her whereabouts while she was gone.

"Keep an eye on her," she said to Jimmy Dale as if I could go anywhere. She went into a bedroom and shut the door. I could only assume she was calling someone for further instructions.

Again the minutes dragged by as I contemplated my situation. I knew I was in extreme trouble. Jimmy Dale slouched on the leather sofa, his right ankle resting on his left knee. He was wearing blue jeans, slung so low on his narrow hips I was afraid he was going to lose them. A faded Grateful Dead T-shirt and thongs completed his outfit. His hair looked as uncombed as it had the first time I'd seen him, and his eyes still held that sleepy look. Maybe it was permanent with him. It probably was the dope, but I'm so naive I wasn't sure how to tell. He chewed on a fingernail and rhythmically slapped the thong bottom against his right foot as if listening to some internal rock beat.

Finally Barb came out of the bedroom. "We have to get her out of here. There'll be too many people around by suppertime."

"Where we takin' her?"

"It's for me to know and you to find out." She sounded like a smug kindergartner taunting her playmate. "I'll go out and make sure no one is around before you bring her out to my car."

She went out the front door and closed it carefully behind her. In a minute she was back. "The coast is clear. Jimmy Dale, untie her feet but leave her hands tied. Here's the knife in case she decides to get cute. Bring along the cord so we can tie her up again in the car. Walk close behind her so if anyone does come by they won't see her hands."

She turned and glared at me. "Don't even think about trying to get away. You saw what happened to Beth. It can happen to you, too." Even though I was frightened out of my mind by now, at least I felt vindicated in my belief in Beth. She had resisted them. Somehow Beth got coerced into the scam and, in the end, tried to get out of it.

Jimmy Dale proceeded to waggle the knife in my

face before laying it down on the coffee table. Then he knelt down and undid the cord around my feet.

When I stood up, Barb came over and frisked me like a criminal suspect. She reached in my slacks pocket and pulled out my car keys. "Which car is yours?"

I said nothing.

"Goddamn it. Jimmy Dale, you know what her car looks like. I want you to follow me in it. We can't leave it here."

"Hell, no, I'm not drivin' that car. The brakes can go at any minute."

"We'll drive slow. You'll be okay."

"Aw, hell, Barb, why d'you always give me the lousy jobs?"

"Because you get paid very well for doing very little. So you do what I tell you to do."

Jimmy Dale sulked but he was no match for Barb, so he picked up the knife and told me to start walking. Barb went ahead of us, opening the front door and checking outside the gate before we went out onto the walk that led past that row of condos. Her station wagon was parked as close to his place as she could get, and she opened the rear door and Jimmy Dale hustled me into the backseat.

"Lie down on the floor," Barb commanded. It is very awkward to get down on the floor of a car when your hands are tied behind your back. I had to lie on the seat and roll off sideways, ending in a jumbled heap. I'd never felt so helpless.

"Tie up her feet again," she told Jimmy Dale, who, as always, complied immediately with her demands.

"Okay, where's her car?" she asked.

There were only four cars in the lot, hers, my rental car and two others.

"It ain't here." Jimmy Dale was very upset at this turn of events.

"Well, she drove here in something. Try the key in all of them till you find one that it fits."

"Sure." He sounded relieved. "At least I won't have to drive the one with bad brakes."

A few minutes passed until I heard him call, "I found it." A door slammed shut and an engine started.

Barb then opened the door of her car and got in. I was lying almost facedown and felt rather than saw her. The seat compressed as she knelt on it, and she cast a shadow over me as she leaned over the back of it to check me out. She must have decided I could do little damage, and she was right.

She sat down, started the engine, turned the radio on to golden oldies and drove out of the parking lot. I felt the burning sensation of acid reflux in my throat as my stomach responded to my terror. Although the air was hot and oppressive on the floor, my whole body was trembling as though a chill wind had just blown across me. That chill wind was blowing through my heart, as well.

TWENTY-ONE

FOR A SHORT TIME I COULD at least speculate on where she was going. I tried to remember right and left turns and estimate distances between them. But soon I lost all sense of direction, time and distance. The transmission hump in the floor was digging into my side and every little bump we hit felt like a jab in the ribs. Not only was my neck throbbing from the way I was lying, but the bindings on my arms and legs were beginning to cut off circulation. I'm sure it was possible to feel worse, but I didn't know how. And the terror seemed to increase the misery tenfold.

I kept hoping someone in an eighteen-wheeler could look down and see me trussed up in the back, but apparently no one was looking or it was too dark on the floor, especially with her tinted windows. Barb had the windows up and the radio turned up loud enough it would have drowned out any calls for help. Besides, although Jimmy Dale had the knife with him, I'd come to the conclusion that Barb was one mean woman, and I knew she wouldn't hesitate to do almost anything to me.

The traffic sounds finally faded almost away, and I could only assume we were out of the city. But in which direction? I couldn't even estimate which direction the sun was since I was lying in the shadows of the floor. I was staring at the underpinnings of the front seat, and my line of vision didn't go much beyond that. The musty smell of carpeting and stale cigarettes was strong enough to make me want to gag. We kept going, though, for what seemed an eternity in my miserably uncomfortable position.

At long last she pulled slowly into someplace dark. I thought it was a garage, but I couldn't tell for sure. After a minute I heard the rumbling of an automatic garage door moving and saw what light there was fade, and knew I was right.

I heard car doors slam and the murmur of voices for several minutes before the back door of the car was opened and Jimmy Dale untied the cord around my ankles. Then he grabbed my right elbow and hauled me, stumbling and light-headed, out of the car. I was so sore and my muscles so cramped, it was all I could do to stand up. He held my right arm firmly, steadying me.

We were in a three-car garage, and Jimmy Dale had pulled my rental car inside beside Barb's. On the other side of the Volvo was a black BMW. Along the front wall was the usual suburban accumulation: riding lawn mower, gardening tools, bicycles and so on. We had to be at someone's home. At Barb's command, Jimmy Dale guided me over to the side door, which led, I assumed, up a couple of steps into the house. He opened the door for me, and the three of us stepped into a large and finely appointed kitchen. With beautifully crafted cherry cabinets, gleaming granite countertops, stainless appliances including a professional quality stove, and a huge island in the middle of the room that featured a second sink, it seemed straight out of the pages of *House Beautiful*. And right beside the door we had just entered, I saw a wall phone with its number listed on a small inserted card that was the same number as the slip of paper in my purse. It had been branded on my brain since I'd been so curious about it.

Leaning casually on a corner of the island was a man who looked familiar, but I couldn't immediately place him. And then it clicked. It was Steve Eberhart who'd been at Jean's dinner party, one half of the couple who'd seemed so in love.

"You three are in this together?" It was an idiotic question, but I was giddy with apprehension.

"You might say we're business partners," Steve said pleasantly as though we were continuing our conversation from the dinner party. That made what he said all the more disquieting. "We like to help widows 'invest' their insurance proceeds in creative endeavors."

"Like a fake kidnapping."

"Yes, I'm extremely proud of that one. That was our most imaginative venture."

"Just like Disney World," I said sarcastically. "And how did you manage to get Beth involved?" By this time I was so wired with anxiety my mouth seemed to have a will of its own.

Steve rubbed his hands together like a chef expounding on the remarkable qualities of his most famous entrée. "That was the only time we recruited an outsider. We needed someone young with a sterling reputation who would be convincing. Beth was a wonderful candidate. And she very wisely agreed to cooperate with us rather than have her family informed of the fact that she posed nude at the art school and that she had an abortion. We had irrefutable evidence we could have shown them. Admittedly, she was a reluctant candidate, and unfortunately, in the end, she had a last-minute change of heart and was going to return your money."

"And so you killed her."

"She had an unfortunate accident."

Barb looked at him sharply. "Haven't you already said more than enough, Steve? You don't have to spill your guts to her."

He shrugged casually. "What difference does it make? She's not going to tell anyone. You and your cousin have had several opportunities to take care of it, but unfortunately, due to his ineptitude, that didn't work out."

I was sure my heart was going to stop. I thought of Mark at home, probably still asleep, waking to find my note that I'd gone to do some errands. How long would it take before he started worrying about me? I thought of Cal and our conversation about leaving the investigation to the police. I'd never dreamed what I was getting into when I went to Yeoman Life. It seemed like a lead I needed to track down, and I didn't feel I was taking a risk. What could be more innocuous than going to a life insurance office? Of course, following Barb wasn't exactly the smartest thing I'd ever done. And now it seemed I was going to pay for it with my life.

"Okay, Jimmy Dale, bring her along," Steve said, heading out of the kitchen. He led the way down a hallway that gave me a glimpse of the dining room and foyer, which were beautifully furnished in what appeared to be exquisite antiques. We came to a small windowless half bath, with a sink and toilet in a room that measured about four by six.

"Sit her on the can and tie her ankles again," he ordered. Jimmy Dale had brought along the extension cord he'd taken off in the garage and roughly tied me up again.

"Jimmy Dale will be sitting right outside the door, so don't think you're going anywhere. If you start giving us trouble, we can easily fix it so you won't bother us."

Barb was hanging around watching all this but had little to say. Finally she spoke to Steve. "When does Liz get back?"

"Not until tomorrow night. Emma here will be long gone before then. Don't worry about Liz finding out."

So Liz apparently didn't know what they were doing. A case of playacting on Steve's part. Had he taught Beth how to seem sincere when telling a lie? The world seemed rife with counterfeit personalities.

When they closed the door, the darkness was palpable. Not a shred of light shone under the door, thanks to the lushness of the thick pile carpeting in the hall.

I'm not ordinarily afraid of the dark, but sitting on that commode, my future looking as bleak as possible, the blackness became my nemesis, filled with terrors that I'd never before encountered. Time became distorted. With nothing to gauge it against, I could no longer calculate the passage of a minute or an hour. The dread kept building within me, layer upon layer, and I knew what it must feel like to be paranoid, to be in constant fear. It truly was a living hell.

To add to my misery, pain was radiating up and down my spine from having to sit the way I was, no backrest with the low-profile toilet, seat hard as stone.

IT MUST HAVE BEEN MANY hours later when the door opened, and the three of them were standing in the hall, looking at me. It took a few minutes for my eyes to adjust to the light.

"Well, I see you're still with us," Steve said so smugly I'd have spit in his face if I could have spit that far. "We're going for another ride."

We went through the routine of untying my ankles again; I guess neither of the men felt like carrying me. When we got to the kitchen, I realized it was dark out and rain was making a drumroll on the kitchen skylights. They hurried me out into the garage and back into Barb's car. Facedown on the floor, of course, my feet trussed up again. I could tell from their voices that Steve got into the driver's seat, and Barb sat in the passenger seat. From what I could tell, Jimmy Dale was going to drive my rental car again.

The garage door went up, and we backed out into the downpour. As we drove along, I heard little traffic noise. It was my impression that it was very late and few people were on the road.

After considerable internal debate, I decided I wanted to know what I faced. Somehow it seemed easier to deal with than letting my imagination go full tilt.

"Please tell me what you're going to do with me," I said, feeling as though I was talking to the carpet. "That's the least you can do."

"Sure, why not?" said Steve. "Anticipation is nine-tenths of the fun, isn't it? It's a nasty, rainy night out. It's hard to see and the roads are slick. You're going to lose control of your car at that spot just to the side of the Siesta Drive bridge where the fishermen like to park, and you're going to drive right into the Intracoastal waterway."

Dear God. Could they have known how much I fear water? I can't swim, and I panic when I can't touch the bottom. They couldn't possibly have chosen a more terrifying method of death for me. The only thing I could hope for was to die of fright or a heart attack before the car sank.

When we finally reached our destination, we sat there for a while before they finally got me out of the car again. It was still raining hard, and as I became soaked, I began to shiver, though my shivering had little to do with being cold. Barb was under an umbrella, but she didn't offer to hold it over me. Though it was forbiddingly dark, I could make out that we were parked just off the road near the bridge, and Jimmy Dale had parked my car headed toward the water, its front wheels a couple of feet from the ground-level retaining wall that kept the parking lot from washing away.

"Okay, Emma," Steve said. "Let's get you in your car." My hands were still tied behind my back. I wondered if there was anything I could do when they finally untied them, but since there were three of them and one of me, it didn't seem at all likely. When I reached the car, Jimmy Dale undid my wrists, and my arms hung numbly at my sides. I wasn't sure I could even open the car door, let alone attempt to get away.

Steve opened the door and, bowing like a doorman, said, "Please get in." When I balked, Jimmy Dale roughly grabbed my left arm above the elbow and forced me into the seat. Then he picked up my feet and shoved them inside.

"Is her purse in there?" Steve asked Jimmy Dale. "We want to make sure it looks like she simply lost control."

"Yeah, it's in the backseat where she left it," he replied. I remembered now that I'd left it on the floor in back when I'd parked at Northgate Commons. Well, at least they would be able to identify my body when they fished it out of the waterway.

Steve slammed the door shut, and it wasn't till then that I realized the motor was running and the transmission was in Drive. I tried frantically to put it in Park, but it wouldn't go; something had been crammed into the slot that kept me from moving the lever either way. I could only assume that whatever it was, it would be

water soluble and would be gone by the time anyone
found the car.

I tried the door handle, only to have it fall off in my
hand. I reached across to the other door, but it had been
tampered with, too. I suppose Steve reasoned that when
the forensics team investigated my death, they would
assume I broke the handle off in my panic to get out
of the car. The buttons that made the windows go up
and down didn't work, either. I was a prisoner. And my
prison was to be my tomb.

Suddenly I felt something shoving the car. I looked in
the rearview mirror and realized it was Steve in Barb's
car. I managed to put my foot on the brake and push as
hard as I could, although I felt as though all my strength
had abandoned me. But the movement forward was in-
exorable. My front wheels dropped into the water, and
I could hear a scraping noise as the underside of the car
was pushed across the stone wall. Shortly the car tipped
forward into the water, and then the rear end fell off the
edge. I watched in horror as the water came up to the
hood, inching its way toward the windshield. My car
was totally in the water now, sinking fast, and Steve
and the others were back on dry land.

They say your whole life goes before your eyes when
you're about to die. And that's God's truth. Flashes of
incidents from childhood on went by in fast-forward:
moments of joy like Mark's birth, and moments of despair like Paul's death. I wondered if Mark could handle
all he'd been through this year: the death of his father,
all the problems he had with Cindy and now this. I was

afraid my death would utterly destroy him. That more than any other fact made me realize that it was imperative to survive this situation. My son needed me.

My only chance was to break a window. I figured I had a few minutes before the water would start filling up the car, and somehow during those few minutes I'd have to get out the window. I'd deal with the fact I couldn't swim after that.

What the hell would I break it with? If it had been my own car, there would have been a flashlight in the glove compartment. But rental cars have only paperwork. Then I remembered my purse—and my umbrella. When I moved to Florida, Mark gave me a compact folding umbrella that had a heavy metal handle. He was only half kidding when he said, "Mom, God knows what kind of crazies you might run into down there. This is small enough to fit in your shoulder bag, but that handle can be pretty lethal. You might be able to fend off some mugger with it."

I'd laughed at him at the time and told him he was unnecessarily paranoid. And I didn't carry it all the time. Only when it rained. Thank God they'd forecasted rain for today. Or was that yesterday?

I twisted around and knelt on the seat to reach my bag on the back floor. By now the water had nearly covered the windshield. I'm not usually claustrophobic, but I had the strong sensation that my space was getting smaller and smaller and closing in on me. Propelled by urgency and fear, I sat back down and rummaged hurriedly through the bag. The umbrella was in the bottom, just where I'd stashed it. The three of them must not have gone through the purse, assuming there was no point to it. They wanted everything to look as normal as possible when the car was found.

I clutched the umbrella with both hands and used the metal handle like a battering ram, slamming it against the window. It bounced off. I knew it would be a matter of seconds before the car was completely underwater. I thought I could hear the faint sounds of the undulating waves and knew it was the sound of death.

A sheer rage took hold of me then. How could they do this to me? Those sons of bitches were greedy bastards who'd already taken one life. By God, they weren't going to take mine, too!

I was mindless with fury. I pounded again and again at the recalcitrant window, willing every ounce of energy I had into the task, until finally it shattered into a million pieces, and a cascade of seawater knocked me backward onto the seat. I took a giant breath and, working against the tremendous force of the water, managed to slowly squirm out of the window. I paddled upward the best I knew how and found myself on the roof of the car. As I stood up on it, my head broke the surface, and I opened my mouth and took in deep gasps of fresh, sweet air. Apparently the water was shallow enough here that the roof of the car was only a few feet below the surface.

It wasn't until I'd caught my breath that I began to worry about being seen by my abductors. But there was no one in sight. It was pouring even harder now, and the three of them were apparently so convinced I couldn't escape, they'd left before someone questioned what they were doing there. They wouldn't have wanted any wandering patrol cars to drive by or other passing cars to place them at the scene.

I gauged the distance to shore to be about twenty yards. I wanted to get to the sloping sandy area beyond the retaining wall because I wasn't sure I had the strength to pull myself up over it. As terrified as I was, I knew that if I put my mind to it, I could dog-paddle that far. For sure I wasn't going to stand on the roof of the car until daybreak. And I was worried that the car would drift farther out in the water. That thought frightened me more than trying to swim.

I waited a few minutes to reassure myself that they all were really gone. Then I took another deep breath and pushed myself off from the car. I paddled furiously, my fear propelling my arms like windmills, and just when I thought I wasn't going to make it, my foot touched bottom.

TWENTY-TWO

I WAS SOAKED, I WAS shivering with cold and I was ecstatic! I had survived!

My mind wasn't functioning at its highest level, and I couldn't think what to do next. There was no one around at this hour, especially not in this downpour. If I didn't get dry, I thought, I'd end up with pneumonia. I finally decided to walk toward Osprey Avenue. If I was going to find any help, it would probably be there or another block east on the Trail.

It was only a few blocks, but with the rain pummeling me, my clothes clinging cold against my skin and my shoes feeling like wet seaweed tied to my feet, it seemed much farther. I was hugging myself, trying to keep from shivering so hard, staring down at the sidewalk to keep the rain out of my eyes. I never wanted to be home in my own warm bed so much in my life.

I stood on the corner of Osprey for probably fifteen minutes, wondering if I should keep walking to try and find an all-night bar or store, when I saw headlights coming toward me from the north. I waved, rather feebly, I suspect, and a taxi pulled up beside me. The driver, a skinny middle-aged black man, got out and came around to me.

"Lawd, ma'am, you okay?" His face showed great concern.

"I'll be okay if you'll just take me home." I tried but couldn't stop shivering as I spoke.

He took off his baseball jacket and held it out to me. "Whyn't you put this on before you gets your death?"

"I hate to get it all wet for you."

He opened the back door of the cab. "You cain't hurt it. Best put it on. Hurry and get in before you get more soaked."

It was impossible to get more soaked, but I gratefully climbed into the cab and huddled in the jacket without putting my arms in the sleeves. At least I wouldn't get them all wet. I gave him my address and lay back against the seat in utter exhaustion. He asked no questions, and I wasn't going to try to explain my situation. I knew I'd have to do that many times over before I was done.

When he pulled up to the front door at La Hacienda, I explained I'd lost my purse and asked him to wait while I went up to my condo and sent down my son to pay him.

"Tha's fine. Don't get too many calls this time of night, so they's no rush."

I folded his jacket and handed it to him. I tried to summon a smile, but my teeth were chattering too much to do it. "Thanks for letting me use it."

He nodded and looked concerned. "Glad to. You gets yourself dry and warm, hear?"

I made a wet trail as I entered the lobby. A security

guard always sits inconspicuously at a desk in the corner at night, and his eyes grew wide when he saw me. "You okay?" he asked as he started to rise.

"I will be, Jim, when I get out of these clothes. Just had a little mishap." I waved him back down in his seat.

I took the elevator to eleven, and when I got to my door I found it unlocked.

All of the lights were on, and Mark was sitting on the couch, staring into space. His face looked ravaged. I could only imagine what he'd been going through. The moment he heard me, he jumped to his feet and rushed to me. "Mom, my God!" He gathered me in his arms, soaking his own clothes, and held me tight. "Jesus! I was afraid you were dead."

Then he held me at arm's length and looked me up and down. "I've been out of my mind. The police are looking for you. What the hell happened?"

"I need fifteen minutes," I pleaded. "I'm chilled to the bone. I want to take a hot bath and put on dry clothes. Then I'll tell you the whole thing. Okay?"

"All right. But I'm going to call the police and tell them you're home."

"Why don't you have someone come over here. That way I'll only have to tell my story once. But before you do that, there's a taxi driver waiting downstairs to be paid. I lost my purse, so I told him you'd pay him."

"Go get in the tub. I'll go down right now."

The hot bath felt so wonderful I nearly fell asleep in the bathtub. And I wondered if anyone had ever drowned doing just that. Wouldn't that have been ironic?

When I got out, I dressed in a pair of blue jeans and a sweatshirt. I knew I wasn't going to get any sleep tonight. I hadn't had anything to eat since noon, and my body was telling me it was time for some sustenance. Mark confessed he hadn't eaten, either, as he'd been so upset, so I made turkey, cucumber and cream cheese sandwiches and got a couple of beers.

Since he knew I was waiting to tell my story when the police arrived, he told me about his day after he awoke to find me gone.

"Of course I found your note. But when it got to be suppertime and you weren't back, I got really concerned. By eight I called the cops. I knew it wasn't like you, and after those incidents with both our cars and you nearly getting run down in the restaurant parking lot, I figured there had to be something really wrong. I guess I'm a little slow, but, Mom, you kept reassuring me. When will I ever learn not to listen to you?"

I felt terrible deceiving Mark the way I had, even more so now that he was aware of it. "I'm sorry, honey. It's just that I know what a worrywart you are. And you've had so much on your mind lately. I didn't want to add to your burden." God, but that sounded lame.

He scrubbed his forehead with the heels of his hands. "So you wait until something terrible happens to you. Do you think that makes me feel any better? I thought we were supposed to be there for each other."

I took his hand. "Next time…"

"I think I've heard that before," he interrupted. "Now, I'll go nuts if you don't tell me…"

"The police should be here very soon, Mark. Don't make me go through it twice."

We said little more, and, thankfully, the police did arrive soon after that. In fact, it was Detective Caronis and another man he introduced as Detective Slidell.

I told them every detail I could think of from the time I left home until I returned. Then I filled them in on all the people I'd talked to about Beth and how I came to suspect Yeoman Life had some connection. Mark sat there quietly, but I could tell from his expression that he was very disturbed by it all.

Dawn was beginning to lighten the sky by the time the detectives left. I could finally let down, and a terrible exhaustion swept over me, made doubly powerful from a lethal combination of physical and emotional trauma. I felt like I could sleep for a week. But first I had to square things with Mark—again.

"Now you know there was more to it than just not burdening you with my problems," I said. "You have to understand how mortified I was about losing that money. How could I tell you about the whole situation without confessing that?"

"I would have understood."

"You would have freaked out, Mark, and you know it. And I felt I was breaking an unspoken pact I had with your father's memory—not to fritter away the money he worked so hard to accumulate for my well-being."

"What about Cal? He apparently knew."

"That was kind of a fluke," I said. And sharing with him I'd lost the money was easier than telling Mark.

Friends can take an objective view; kids are not likely to. "I made all the decisions," I went on. "The only reason he went to Miami with me was because I'd said I'd do something with him that day and then had to beg off. I felt I owed him, and he offered to help drive to Miami."

"You'd tell him and not me," Mark said, pouting the way he had as a child.

"That's the whole point, Mark. You're my son. I love you dearly. And believe me, I didn't mean to put myself in danger. I had no earthly idea when I left the house yesterday that I would find myself in such a situation. I'd never do that to you knowingly."

"Well…" Mark took my hand. "I've got to say you've got a lot of guts, Mom. And I guess I sort of understand…in a way." He said it grudgingly, and I hoped he meant it.

He gave me a bear hug. "But," he added, "please don't do that again. You're making an old man out of me."

TWENTY-THREE

I PROBABLY COULD HAVE slept around the clock, but I awoke in the late afternoon because I was hungry again.

"You've had three calls," Mark told me. "Jean Jacobs and Cal and Detective Caronis called. I said you'd call them back."

I called Caronis first.

"We've got all three of them," he said, "and Jimmy Dale is ratting them all out. Several other people are involved, too, and we have warrants out for them. It was a big operation. Barb Jacobs was one of two insurance employees who gave them names of widows who'd received large insurance payments within the past year. They liked to wait a few months so their schemes wouldn't arouse suspicion that they were linked to life insurance payouts. Yeoman Life's management was appalled when they found out what had been going on. In fact, they plan to make restitution to all who've been duped. Steven Eberhart and a couple of others planned and ran the scams."

"He concocted the fake-kidnapping plot?"

"Yeah. They got really carried away with that. Jimmy Dale only recently got involved with them, and when he told Barbara about loaning money to Tim for Beth's

abortion and her parents' fundamentalist views, Steve
came up with the plan. Apparently it worked out beautifully until the very end. When Beth met Jimmy Dale
that day with the money, the enormity of what she'd
done must have hit her, and she tried to talk him into
skipping town with her and sending the money back to
you."

"I never could picture her as a greedy opportunist.
From what everyone said, it was completely out of character for her to do anything like that."

"Apparently she was so afraid of her parents' reaction to her so-called sins, Steve and Barbara were able
to manipulate her into doing something totally foreign
to her standards. Unfortunately, though, her change of
heart at the last minute cost her her life. Jimmy Dale
called Steve, and the two of them took her to a marina
and forced her at gunpoint into a boat that Steve took far
enough out into the Gulf that she couldn't swim back.
Jimmy Dale followed them in a second boat, which they
abandoned after throwing Beth overboard. When they
came back to shore, they decided to leave those packets of money in the water so it would look more like an
accidental drowning."

"How did Beth know who I was the morning she
pointed me out to Tom on the beach? I'd spoken to her
casually, but I'd never given her my name."

"They'd set up a spotter. Evidently, your friend Jean
Jacobs had casually mentioned to her daughter-in-law
once that you'd been going out on the beach every morning since your husband died. They had someone hang-

ing out on the eleventh floor that day pretending to do some maintenance. When you came out of your condo, he called Beth at the restaurant next-door and described what you were wearing so she could pick you out on the beach. They'd thought of everything. If you hadn't pursued it so aggressively, we would probably never have unscrambled it."

"You're not implying that Jean Jacobs was involved."

"Not at all. It was an innocent remark that they cleverly used for their purposes."

"My name isn't going to come up in this, is it? As far as the media are concerned, I mean?"

"When it was just the scam, no. But now it's attempted murder. I'm afraid there's no way to keep your name out of it."

"Oh, damn."

"Sorry. We'll do what we can. But be prepared."

After filling Mark in on all this, I called Jean. Had she already heard about it? How would she feel when she knew what her daughter-in-law had done to me?

The minute I identified myself, her words came pouring out in a torrent. "Oh, Emma, you know how I've felt about my daughter-in-law. I knew there was something terribly wrong there, but I couldn't put my finger on it. She's been arrested! Can you believe that? Something about fraud and attempted murder! Oh, poor Sam. He's just devastated. And that couple who was here that night for dinner? It seems Steve was involved, too. I'd only met them once, but Barbara had asked me to have them over sometime. She said they were interested in buying a condo at the beach and wanted to know what La Hacienda was like."

"Jean—" I finally got a word in edgewise "—I'm afraid it's even worse than you know. I wouldn't say anything, but it's going to be in the papers, so…"

"Emma, what on earth? How do you know anything about this?"

How could I put it to soften the impact? I decided it was impossible. "I was their victim, Jean. Beth was blackmailed into drawing me into a fake kidnapping story. I gave her money for the so-called 'ransom' for her nonexistent grandmother."

There was a momentary silence while Jean absorbed all this. "Oh, my God, Emma. What can I say? My own daughter-in-law…" I could tell she was in tears.

"Listen, Jean, I want to make this very plain. It has nothing whatsoever to do with you. I value your friendship way too much to let it be affected by this."

"But, Emma, it was my family…"

"Only by marriage, and soon she won't be part of it at all."

We talked a little longer until I hoped I'd convinced her that Barb's actions would not change our relationship. I knew that as the details of my ordeal were published, she would be mortified, but I'd do everything I could to convince her that I still cherished her friendship.

Finally I called Cal and asked him to come over. I owed him more than a phone call.

Mark excused himself to walk on the beach when Cal arrived, giving us a chance for a private conversation.

"I have a confession to make," I told him after pouring each of us a glass of chardonnay. "I got caught up in tracking down the people involved in the scam though I told you I'd leave it to the police."

"Emma, that was dangerous. Why did you do that?"

"It was kind of an accident. I thought what I was doing was perfectly safe. It turned out to be anything but." And then I told him, in detail, the events of the day before.

He was horrified, of course. "You shouldn't have…"

"Look, I've just been through this same discussion with Mark. Perhaps what I did was foolish, but I'm my own person and have a right to make my own decisions, Cal. If anything, all this has taught me I can be pretty resourceful when the chips are down."

Cal stared down into his wine as if there were a message there for him. Finally he looked up and smiled. He raised his glass in a toast and said, "Here's to a friend who's got more class and more balls, if you'll excuse the expression, than most anyone I know, male or female. I'm really impressed."

That was one of the nicest compliments I've ever had.

* * * * *

REQUEST YOUR FREE BOOKS!

2 FREE NOVELS
PLUS 2 FREE GIFTS!

MYSTERY **WORLDWIDE LIBRARY**®
Your Partner in Crime

They made their way across the pasture toward the chapel. Vi and Delia kept craning their necks, exclaiming at the rugged terrain. "You can see for miles out here," Delia avowed. "It does look like the earth touches the sky. What a fantastic place. I never knew anything like this existed."

"Are there really Indian tribes out here?" Vi peered around her as though expecting to see an Indian village pop out of the open field.

"I think so," Ada replied distantly. It was actually the furthest thing from her mind at the moment. "I don't know for certain. We shall have to ask Jack."

"I like it here," replied Vi. "I think we should stay. What do you think, Delia?"

"I agree." Delia smiled at her eldest sister. "It will be nice to be one big family again."

"Jack has already said that you may stay if you want to." Ada patted both of her sisters. "He thinks that New York is no place for a civilized young woman to live."

The carriage traced a semicircle in front of the chapel and drew to a halt. The sisters gasped excitedly at the sight of it.

The chapel was beautiful and had been since the day they put the final coat of paint on it. Today, however, it was touched with majesty and grandeur. It gleamed, as pure and white as a string of pearls against the deep azure sky. The spire seemed to touch the heavens. As she gazed at the chapel, a deep feeling of peace and intense joy stole over her. No matter what happened, she and Jack would face life together. Their families would be with them the whole time.

She would never be alone to face the world again.

She had thought she had the world figured out and

that she could be responsible for every person under her care. What she had found, however, was that much of life had to be taken on faith, and that only by dedicating her heart to God could she begin to understand the depth of love she had for others.

Vi and Delia embraced her once more, and Vi fussed with her veil, and then they scurried inside the chapel to find their seats. The Stillmans congratulated her, and Mr. Stillman gave Laura a coin and then they, too, went inside the chapel. It was just Laura and Ada alone, waiting to go in.

The wind whipped her veil around her head, and she held it close with her free hand.

Laura turned to her. "Are you nervous?"

Ada smiled. "I was. I don't think I am any longer."

"That's good." Laura took her hand in hers. "C'mon, Ma. Let's go."

Ada gasped with joy as Laura pushed open the heavy oak door of the chapel. The entire assembled population of Winchester Falls rose as they walked in.

Laura led her down the aisle, presenting Ada to her father with the same aplomb she would use to bestow a gift. As they joined hands, Ada leaned close to him.

"She called me Ma," she whispered. "My cup of joy runneth over."

Jack smiled at her, a tender expression in his eyes. "She called me Pa," he whispered back. "My daughter has finally come home."

They stood before Reverend Caussey and repeated their vows, affirming their love for and dedication to each other and the Lord. They were in the company of their family and their town, and she could not ask for a more auspicious beginning to their real marriage. Gathered under this roof were the people who mattered most.

The ceremony was over in a whirlwind of applause and kisses and shaking of hands. Ada marched out of the chapel on her handsome husband's arm, shielding her face with her hand as the bright radiance of the midafternoon sun hit her full force.

After the wedding luncheon, served by Maggie and Cathy and Mrs. H., a group of musicians from the town assembled under the trees and struck up a few chords. Jack led her out onto the platform they had hastily assembled for dancing and swung her along with a lilting waltz.

"This is the first time we've danced together," he remarked. "I can't believe I waited this long."

Ada laughed. "I can't believe it, either. Waltzing used to be a regular pastime of mine. When I wasn't marching in parades, of course."

"Do you miss your life in New York?" He gazed down into her eyes.

"My life now is real and vital," she responded. It was the simple truth. "When I was living in my father's home, it's hard to describe, but everything seemed to be a mere theory. As though I were simply spouting a philosophy of how I wanted to live or what I wanted to be. When I came here, though, life was no longer merely theoretical. I had to learn to do rather than to say. There is a rough kind of equality to life out here, isn't there?"

"I would agree to that." He swooped her around another turn. "Does it make you happy?"

She gazed up at her husband, so tall and so handsome and so infinitely wonderful that she caught her breath a little. "Happier than I have any right to be."

A little scuffle sounded above the music, and Jack halted their dance. They turned to see the cause of the commotion.

A group of townspeople had started arguing vociferously. One of the men was the little old man with the bushy beard, who had been part of the throng outside the post office when she went to send the telegram. "Well, I don't care what y'all say. We ought to have a fire department. The first time that a fire starts up on the prairie, you'll be wishing for one. Why we didn't have a fire in the midst of that tornado, I don't know. But we need one. We're a proper town with a proper chapel."

The townspeople murmured and muttered, turning to each other for confirmation. "Well, I don't see the point of having a fire department if we don't have a mayor." One of the other men banged his fist on the wooden picnic table. "Until we get a mayor, no fire department."

Stella Cotton broke free from her dancing partner and stood on top of a picnic table. "I think Ada Burnett oughta be our mayor," she hollered. "Miz Burnett sure did help us after the twister, and she knew how to handle those reporters."

"Here, here!" Mr. Pollitt banged on the picnic table.

An excited murmur ran through the crowd. Ada turned to Jack. "I don't know what to say. Mayor?" She had always dreamed of holding political office, but of course, that had to wait until women got the vote. Didn't it?

Jack gave his loud whistle, the one that stopped all

activity. Everyone paused to look at the couple standing, hand in hand, on the dance floor. Some, possibly a little shamefaced at breaking up Ada and Jack's
wedding dance, looked uncomfortably at the ground.

"As y'all know, my wife helped put the town back
together after the twister hit because she knows how to
organize people and how to play to people's strengths.
Like y'all said, she knows how to handle the press.
She's also right smart about politics, and she's brave."
He smiled down at her encouragingly, the corners of
his green eyes wrinkling. "Well, if y'all want her and
she wants the job, I reckon you couldn't do better." He
turned to Ada. "Do you want the job?"

Ada nodded, her eyes glowing like stars.

"All right," the old man with the beard shouted.
"We'll elect her mayor, and then we'll draw up our
town charter. Winchester Falls will be on the map
at last."

"All in favor?" Someone in the back of the throng
called.

A resounding "aye" welled up from the assembled
crowd, followed by catcalls and whistles. Ada burst
into laughter, tears coming to her eyes. So many things
had happened in the space of just a few short hours.
She had become Laura's ma. She had married her
husband in truth. Now she was mayor of Winchester
Falls, the best little town in Texas.

"I hope that was okay with you," Jack whispered,
bending down close. "I just knew you were right for
the job."

"Perfect," she managed to respond before the next
roar from the crowd.

"Mayor, we need a fire department," the little man

bellowed, standing up on the picnic table to be heard above the crowd.

"Now, now." Ada yelled as loud as she could to be heard above the fray. "We'll meet tomorrow evening at the ranch—around seven o'clock. Now, we need to celebrate. Let's dance."

Everyone broke into applause as Jack led her out onto the dance floor to resume their waltz. Ada beamed up at her husband as they whirled around in time to the music.

She was no longer living in theory. She was living in fact.

She could not thank God enough for all He had given her.

* * * * *

Dear Reader,

This is my first Western story ever, and I hope you liked it. My family and I recently moved from the Dallas–Fort Worth metroplex to a small, almost ghost town near Wichita Falls. We awaken to the sounds of our neighbor's horses neighing or to the sound of windmill blades whining in the strong Texas wind. We are restoring a small 1920s bungalow. To say this has been a family adventure would be an understatement!

The experiences we've had out here have formed the backdrop for my story about Ada Westmore, Jack Burnett and his daughter, Laura. Even the little church they built is modeled on one that is right next door to us. It was built by Czech immigrants in 1916, and it's where we attend services on Sunday morning. In a way, it's a place where time has stood still, and I am so blessed to be living here and to be sharing stories about this land with you.

In Christ,
Lily George

REQUEST YOUR FREE BOOKS!

2 FREE INSPIRATIONAL NOVELS
PLUS 2 *FREE* MYSTERY GIFTS

Love Inspired® HISTORICAL

YES! Please send me 2 FREE Love Inspired® Historical novels and my 2 FREE mystery gifts (gifts are worth about $10). After receiving them, if I don't wish to receive any more books, I can return the shipping statement marked "cancel." If I don't cancel, I will receive 4 brand-new novels every month and be billed just $4.99 per book in the U.S. or $5.49 per book in Canada. That's a saving of at least 17% off the cover price. It's quite a bargain! Shipping and handling is just 50¢ per book in the U.S. and 75¢ per book in Canada.* I understand that accepting the 2 free books and gifts places me under no obligation to buy anything. I can always return a shipment and cancel at any time. Even if I never buy another book, the two free books and gifts are mine to keep forever.

102/302 IDN GH6Z

Name	(PLEASE PRINT)	
Address		Apt. #
City	State/Prov.	Zip/Postal Code

Signature (if under 18, a parent or guardian must sign)

Mail to the **Reader Service:**
IN U.S.A.: P.O. Box 1867, Buffalo, NY 14240-1867
IN CANADA: P.O. Box 609, Fort Erie, Ontario L2A 5X3

Want to try two free books from another series?
Call 1-800-873-8635 or visit www.ReaderService.com.

* Terms and prices subject to change without notice. Prices do not include applicable taxes. Sales tax applicable in N.Y. Canadian residents will be charged applicable taxes. Offer not valid in Quebec. This offer is limited to one order per household. Not valid for current subscribers to Love Inspired Historical books. All orders subject to credit approval. Credit or debit balances in a customer's account(s) may be offset by any other outstanding balance owed by or to the customer. Please allow 4 to 6 weeks for delivery. Offer available while quantities last.

Your Privacy—The Reader Service is committed to protecting your privacy. Our Privacy Policy is available online at www.ReaderService.com or upon request from the Reader Service.

We make a portion of our mailing list available to reputable third parties that offer products we believe may interest you. If you prefer that we not exchange your name with third parties, or if you wish to clarify or modify your communication preferences, please visit us at www.ReaderService.com/consumerschoice or write to us at Reader Service Preference Service, P.O. Box 9062, Buffalo, NY 14240-9062. Include your complete name and address.

LIH15

SPECIAL EXCERPT FROM

Love Inspired® HISTORICAL

*When a bachelor rancher abruptly gains custody
of his twin nieces, he needs all the help he can get.
But as he starts to fall for the girls' widowed caretaker,
can love blossom for this unexpected family?*

Read on for a sneak preview of
STAND-IN RANCHER DADDY,
the heartwarming beginning of the series
***LONE STAR COWBOY LEAGUE:
THE FOUNDING YEARS***

At last, CJ thought. Help was on the way.

With each step Molly took in his direction, he felt the tension draining out of him. She was a calming influence and the stability they all needed—not just Sarah and Anna, but CJ, too.

If she ever left him…

Not the point, he told himself.

She looked uncommonly beautiful this morning in a blue cotton dress with a white lace collar and long sleeves. The cut of the garment emphasized her tiny waist and petite frame.

He attempted to swallow past the lump in his throat without much success. Molly took his breath away.

If he were from a different family…

"Miss Molly," Anna called out. "Miss Molly, over here! We're over here."

Sarah wasn't content with merely waving. She pulled her hand free of CJ's and raced to meet Molly across the small expanse of grass. Anna followed hard on her sister's heels.

Molly greeted both girls with a hug and a kiss on the top of their heads.

"Well, look who it is." She stepped back and smiled down

at the twins. "My two favorite girls in all of Little Horn, Texas. And don't you look especially pretty this morning."

"Unca Corny picked out our dresses," Sarah told her.

"He tried to make breakfast." Anna swayed her shoulders back and forth with little-girl pride. "He didn't do so good. He burned the oatmeal and Cookie had to make more."

Molly's compassionate gaze met his. "Sounds like you had an…interesting morning."

CJ chuckled softly. "Though I wouldn't want to repeat the experience anytime soon, we survived well enough."

"Miss Molly, look. I'm wearing my favorite pink ribbon." Sarah touched the floppy bow with reverent fingers. "I tied it all by myself."

"You did a lovely job." Under the guise of inspecting the ribbon, Molly retied the bow, then moved it around until it sat straight on the child's head. "Pink is my favorite color."

"It's Pa's favorite, too." Sarah's gaze skittered toward the crowded tent. "I wore it just for him."

The wistful note in her voice broke CJ's heart. He shared a tortured look with Molly.

Her ragged sigh told him she was thinking along the same lines as he was. His brother always made it to church, a fact the twins had reminded him of this morning.

"Pa says Sunday is the most important day of the week," Sarah had told him, while Anna had added, "And we're never supposed to miss Sunday service. Not ever."

Somewhere along the way, the two had gotten it into their heads that Ned would show up at church today. CJ wasn't anywhere near as confident. If Ned didn't make an appearance, the twins would know that their father was truly gone.

Don't miss
STAND-IN RANCHER DADDY
by Renee Ryan, available July 2016 wherever
Love Inspired® Historical books and ebooks are sold.

www.LoveInspired.com

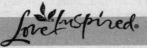
"So you didn't like it here?" Vic asked. "Coming every
summer?"

"I missed my friends back home, but there were parts
I liked."

"I remember seeing you girls in church on Sunday."

"Part of the deal," Lauren said, a faint smile teasing her
mouth. "And I didn't mind that part, either. The message
was always good, once I started really listening. I can't
remember who the pastor was, but what he said resonated
with me."

"Jodie and Erin would attend some of the youth events,
didn't they?"

"Erin more than any of us."

"I remember my brother Dean talking about her," Vic
said. "I think he had a secret crush on her."

"He was impetuous, wasn't he?"

"That's being kind. But he's settled now."

Thoughts of Dean brought up the same problem that
had brought him to the ranch.

His deal with Lauren's father.

"So, I hate to be a broken record," he continued, "but

I was wondering if I could come by the house tomorrow. To go through your father's papers."

Lauren sighed.

Vic tamped down his immediate apology. He had nothing to feel bad about. He was just looking out for his brother's interests.

"Yes. Of course. Though—" She stopped herself there. "Sorry. You probably know better what you're looking for."

Vic shot her a glance across the cab of the truck. "I'm not trying to jeopardize your deal. When I first leased the ranch from your father, it was so that my brother could have his own place. And I'm hoping to protect that promise I made him. Especially now. After his accident."

"I understand," Lauren said, her smile apologetic. "I know what it's like to protect siblings."

"Are you the oldest?"

"Erin and I are twins, but I'm older by twenty minutes."

Lauren smiled at him. And as their eyes held, he felt it again. An unexpected rush of attraction. When her eyes grew ever so slightly wider, he wondered if she felt it, too.

He dragged his attention back to the road.

You're no judge of your feelings, he reminded himself, his hands tightening on the steering wheel as if reining in his attraction to this enigmatic woman.

He'd made mistakes in the past, falling for the wrong person. He couldn't do it again. He couldn't afford to.

Especially not with Lauren.

Don't miss
TRUSTING THE COWBOY
by Carolyne Aarsen, available July 2016 wherever
Love Inspired® books and ebooks are sold.

Reading Has Its Rewards

Earn **FREE BOOKS!**

Register at **Harlequin My Rewards** and submit your Harlequin purchases from wherever you shop to earn points for free books and other exclusive rewards.

Plus submit your purchases from now till May 30th for a chance to win a $500 Visa Card*.

Visit **HarlequinMyRewards.com** today

MYR16R1